SOUP'S
DRUM

OTHER YEARLING BOOKS YOU WILL ENJOY:

SOUP, *Robert Newton Peck*
SOUP AND ME, *Robert Newton Peck*
SOUP FOR PRESIDENT, *Robert Newton Peck*
SOUP ON WHEELS, *Robert Newton Peck*
SOUP IN THE SADDLE, *Robert Newton Peck*
THE GREAT BRAIN, *John D. Fitzgerald*
THE GREAT BRAIN AT THE ACADEMY, *John D. Fitzgerald*
THE GREAT BRAIN REFORMS, *John D. Fitzgerald*
THE GREAT BRAIN DOES IT AGAIN, *John D. Fitzgerald*
HOW TO EAT FRIED WORMS, *Thomas Rockwell*

YEARLING BOOKS/YOUNG YEARLINGS/YEARLING CLASSICS are designed especially to entertain and enlighten young people. Charles F. Reasoner, Professor Emeritus of Children's Literature and Reading, New York University, is consultant to this series.

For a complete listing of all Yearling titles,
write to Dell Readers Service,
P.O. Box 1045, South Holland, Illinois 60473.

Robert Newton Peck

SOUP'S DRUM

Illustrated by Charles Robinson

A Yearling Book

Published by
Dell Publishing
a division of
The Bantam Doubleday Dell Publishing Group, Inc.
1 Dag Hammarskjold Plaza
New York, New York 10017

Yearling ® TM 913705, Dell Publishing a division of
The Bantam Doubleday Dell Publishing Group, Inc.

ISBN: 0-440-40003-1

Reprinted by arrangement with Alfred A. Knopf, Inc.

Printed in the United States of America

June 1988

10 9 8 7 6 5 4 3 2 1

CW

SOUP'S
DRUM

one

"Kissing," said Soup.

When he said the word, it sort of smacked me hard, like when a baseball hits you in the belly. It had a threatening sound.

"Are you sure, Soup?"

"Yup, I'm sure. Girls," said Soup with a worried shake of his head, "are nothing but trouble."

The two of us were dressed up in our good clothes and were walking across Mr. Furdock's pasture toward Norma Jean Bissell's house.

"The way I figure it, Rob, girls never throw a party unless they plan to play a certain game."

"You mean a kissing game?"

"Of course," said Soup. "That's the whole purpose of the party. You just wait and see."

"Look," I told Soup as we climbed up and over the fence, "the way I heard it was that the purpose of the party is to have all of us over to meet Norma Jean's cousin."

"Don't you believe it," said Soup.

"Why not?"

"Because girls are after just one thing."

"Kissing?"

Soup nodded.

"Maybe," I said, "that's why Mama and Aunt Carrie made me take a bath."

"So did *my* mother," said Soup. "The reason she gave me was that a bath would help me make a good impression."

"Maybe she's right, Soup."

"Lately," said Soup, "I sort of decided that my mother knows a few things, and it's just possible that she's a whole lot smarter than I thought she was."

"In what way?"

"Well," said Soup, "about soap and kissing."

Ahead of us was Norma Jean Bissell's house. It was a place I had seen many times, from the outside, where it was safe. But tonight we were going inside, to a party, with *girls*. The imaginary baseball hit my stomach again.

It was a warm evening in June, and the front door was open like a snare. Only the screen door was closed, the one barrier that now separated *my* lips from hers. I could hardly think about Norma Jean Bissell, or look at her in school, without starting to itch. Love, I decided, was a bit like hives.

"Stop scratching," Soup ordered as he knocked on the white edge of the screen door, "or Norma Jean won't believe you took a bath."

I still smelled so soapy that I figured the bath I took would last for darn near the rest of my life.

No one inside had heard Soup's knock. All we could hear was a chorus of girlish giggles, tittering over something. Maybe us. If there were boys inside, there must have been a rule that boys keep quiet at parties. Soup and I were late. The argument I had with Mama about the bath had slowed up my preparation a bit.

"Hi!" said Norma Jean.

She was wearing a white dress with a pink sash, and two pink bows were tied to her pigtails. She had blond hair, blue eyes, and could probably smell soap from at least a mile upwind. I tried to smile, which is very hard to do when you have a baseball in your belly.

"Howdy," said Soup. "We're here."

"Come in, please."

Soup entered first. I followed, to then stand stock-still in the Bissell's parlor. My nose twitched. Norma Jean

Bissell was wearing some sort of lavender perfume, which I hoped would overpower my own brown soapy cloud of Octagon.

Six girls rushed to greet us. Five of them I knew. So did Soup. But the girl with the red hair was a stranger. No doubt she was Norma Jean's cousin, the gal we had been invited over to meet. She was an inch taller than Norma Jean and was missing a front tooth; and her cheeks must have hosted about a million freckles.

"Juliet," said Norma Jean, taking her by the hand in front of Soup and me, "may I present Luther Vinson and Robert Peck."

Soup turned pale.

"And," said Norma Jean, "this is my cousin who just moved to town, Juliet Rapture."

"Charmed," said Juliet.

"Pleased to meet you," I said.

Juliet and I shook hands. As for Soup, he didn't do anything except stare at Norma Jean's cousin, his mouth hanging about as wide open as a Venus-flytrap. For some strange reason, known only to her, Norma Jean threw me a wink as if to tell me that something was going on, that she knew about and I didn't. Yet I had an inkling that, whatever it was, it had plenty to do with Soup Vinson and Juliet Rapture.

"There's punch," said Norma Jean Bissell.

In the dining room, there was. And around the punch bowl, drinking from paper cups, I saw Eddy Tacker, Ally

Tidwell, Rolly McGraw, Wayne Rohlfing, and George Davis.

All the guys said, "Hey." That is, everyone but Soup, who was gaping at Juliet Rapture. Did he think she was pretty? Well, maybe I'd ask.

"Soup?"

No answer . . . Soup was a mile off.

Yeah, I told myself, old Soup sees Juliet as a ripe plum. My pal must have been going blind. It sure was obvious to me that all the girls at the party were uglier than warthogs, save one, Norma Jean Bissell, our hostess. Yet there stood Soup as if his shoes had been nailed to the floor and his brain unplugged.

How, I asked myself, could anyone think that Juliet Rapture was good to look at?

"Are you okay, Soup?"

"Uh . . . sort of."

I whispered, "What's the trouble?"

"You won't believe this, Rob."

"Try me."

"Well," said Soup, "remember the time I got hit in the belly with a baseball that Eddy chucked at me?"

"I recall."

"Right now, I got the same hurt. Only an inch or two higher up."

"Yup," I said, "I know the feeling. Maybe it's gas."

We blew up balloons, got blindfolded to pin a tail on a picture of a jackass, and sang songs that Mrs. Bissell

7

pumped out on the parlor organ. Then we ate. Correction: all of us ate except Soup, who feasted his vision on Juliet Rapture, even though she was missing a front tooth. Her grin was an open garage. When she drank her punch, she jabbed the soda straw through the gap in her mouth. And slurped.

Boy, was she ugly. Soup needed glasses.

Mrs. Bissell kept remarking on how well we *all* were behaving, which pleased me some. I had been warned earlier about the thrashing I would receive from Mama and Papa and Aunt Carrie if I ever got sent home again from a party.

I was also pleased that Janice wasn't there. She was the toughest kid in the school. Janice Riker was the biggest, strongest, meanest kid in Vermont . . . and I was one of her favorite punching bags. Soup could beat me up real easy. But he wouldn't tackle Janice unless he was near starved for punishment.

Mrs. Bissell finally stopped exercising herself and the pump organ. "Say," she said, "it's so balmy tonight, why don't all of you go outside and play Hide and Seek?" She said it right on cue, as if she'd been coached.

We exploded out the door. Boys first, then girls. We were rolling around on the grassy front lawn, all us boys, but the girls stayed up on the porch, whispering.

"Wanna rassle?" asked Eddy Tacker.

"No, thank you," said Norma Jean. "We girls have all decided that maybe there are a few *grown-up* games we can play."

"Like what?" I asked her.

I knew it wouldn't be Indian wrestling, or anything fun, because all seven of the gals wore white dresses and white stockings. And enough satin bows in their hair to supply the ribbon counter at the drygoods store.

"Crack the Whip," suggested Eddy Tacker.

Norma Jean Bissell ignored his suggestion, which I thought would have been some fun, especially with all the mud around. She merely closed her eyes as if she hadn't heard it.

"A new game," she said.

"How do you play it?"

"Now then," said Norma Jean, "everyone count off and be a number."

"Huh?"

"All the boys," she continued, "are even numbers, like 2, 4, 6, 8, and so on . . . and we girls are odd."

"You sure are," said Ally.

Pretending not to listen, Norma Jean said that the girls would take numbers like 1, 3, 5, 7, 9, 11, and 13. If this was going to be something like multiplication, it sure didn't sound very doggone appealing to me. Miss Kelly dished out an hour of arithmetic every day at school, and I sure wasn't hankering for an extra dose. Not at a Friday night party.

I was number 2.

Soup was 4, and when all fourteen of us had numbers, we were told that you weren't allowed to tell your own number to anyone else. Just remember it. So far, it was a real bore, but it sure beat turning the music pages for Mrs. Bissell's singsong. Anything could be more fun than another four verses of "Rock of Ages."

"I'll go first," said Norma Jean.

Walking over to a gap in the sideyard hedge, where there wasn't much light, she turned to say, "And when I call out a number, the boy who took that number has to come behind the bushes and find me. Ready?"

"Okay."

She disappeared, then hollered out, "Two!"

All the girls giggled.

One of them poked me in the ribs, pushing me toward the gap in the shrubbery. This game, whatever it was, had to be related to baseball. My stomach couldn't be wrong.

Knees trembling, I went behind the hedge. That was where I got the surprise of my life. Approaching me, there in the dark, Norma Jean Bissell wrapped her arms around my neck and gave me a calm command.

"Do it."

"What do I do?" I asked her.

"You're supposed to *kiss* me."

I couldn't understand why my voice was shaking worse than my knees, and *her* voice was steadier than her mother's last bass note in "Rock of Ages."

There was only one thing to do, so I up and did it. I kissed Norma Jean Bissell. Placing my lips softly to her cheek, I planted what I thought was a token of affection more adequate than even her wildest expectations.

"Wrong," she whispered.

"What was wrong about it?"

Norma Jean sighed. "You don't have to kiss me on the *cheek*, Rob."

"I don't?"

"No. Try again. And you're supposed to wrap your arms around my waist."

"Like this?"

"A bit tighter."

"Okay. Now what?"

"Well," she said, "*do* it."

I did it. And not on her cheek. It wasn't a whole lot of fun because of all the punch inside me—eight or nine cups. Boy, I really had to *go*.

I almost laughed, remembering that I was number 2.

two

It was Saturday.

Soup had stayed home that morning to do extra chores in order to earn a dime. I did the same. Because, if we hadn't each pocketed a dime by Saturday afternoon, life could have been near to tragic.

By two o'clock, the two of us, along with every other kid in town who could scrape up ten cents, stood in line at the picture show.

"I can hardly wait," said Soup.

"Me neither."

The gates of Heaven finally opened. Forfeiting our dimes, we stampeded into the movie theater, where Soup and I staked our claim to a pair of seats in the very front row. Dead center.

The first film on the double bill was Buck Jones in *Mesa Justice*. It was a breathtaking hour of ranching and rustlers, a black-and-white masterpiece of murderous mayhem that glued our behinds to our seats and our eyes to the giant flickering screen that was almost within a spit away . . . which made it right handy, considering what happened next.

Ally Tidwell threw up.

The second feature, much like the first, was Tom Mix in *Smoking Sixguns*, another hour of outrageous outlaws who were finally roped and hogtied amid constant hoots of approval from Soup and me. And from Ally, whose digestion had been momentarily restored.

But the ringleader of the outlaws got away, and Tom Mix was in pursuit, his trusty lasso looping overhead as he spurred his horse toward a certain conclusion . . .

The film broke.

Revolution ensued. A boo or catcall or hiss erupted from every young throat, except Ally's—he let go another torrent of half-digested popcorn.

"Fix the picture!" Soup was demanding.

Mr. Bartoni, the manager of the theater, hurried up on the stage, trying to explain to his outraged patrons that his projection booth was experiencing a few technical difficulties. Pelted by empty popcorn boxes, lollipop sticks, and paper cups, Mr. Bartoni scurried into the wings. Inch by inch, he fought his way up the aisle, through a barrage of protest, abuse, and hurled debris.

The houselights went on.

"This," said Soup, "is a bad sign."

We redoubled our noise, threatening to pull down the curtain or eat the seats unless Tom Mix returned to us astride his faithful horse, Tony.

Spliced and patched, the film resumed, the houselights dimmed, and relative order was restored. Tom Mix triumphed. As we left the theater, Soup noticed Mr. Bartoni at the drinking fountain, tapping four white tablets out of a bottle labeled Anacin.

"Watch this, Rob," said Soup.

We watched.

I figured Mr. Bartoni's headache must have been a real zinger. No one can hold a pill in his mouth, bend over, and swallow it with a mouthful of water from a drinking fountain. But I'll give Mr. Bartoni credit. He earnestly tried.

"What'll we do now, Soup? We could always take a stroll down to the barbershop and watch Mr. Petty cut hair."

"Or," countered Soup, "we could pop in at the library."

"Until we get kicked out."

"We won't," said Soup. "At least not today."

"How come you want to stop in at the library?"

"Well," said Soup, "I just thought I'd look up a word in a certain book. Let's go."

Across the street, the town library's doors were open. The local librarian, Miss Webster, eyed us with well-founded suspicion, as we rarely entered in search of educational betterment. Yet I liked her ever since she convinced me to read *Ivanhoe*. I figured no one who sponsored a neat guy like Ivanhoe could be all bad. In fact, I went so far as to tell her that I thought Sir Walter Scott just might have a brilliant future.

"May I help you, boys?"

Soup asked, "Miss Webster, do you happen to have a dictionary that we can please use?"

Soup and I had looked up certain words before at the library, and we had often giggled as discovery unfolded and sophistication replaced innocence. The medical dictionary, especially, guarded some rather revealing illustrations, in color.

"What sort of dictionary?"

From the cool edge on Miss Webster's voice, I could tell that neither she nor the library was totally willing to dispense graphic enlightenment without adult supervision.

"Oh," said Soup, "I don't guess it has to be one of your special dictionaries. A usual kind will do."

"Then you wish to look up a *word*."

"Yes'm. Just a word."

"Which one?"

"Well," said Soup, "it *is* sort of personal."

"I see," came the icy ray of understanding.

"Miss Kelly always tells us," Soup explained, "that if you don't understand the complete meaning of a word, then it's best to look it up."

We had learned that invoking the revered name of our teacher, Miss Kelly, was the key that would slide open the bolt to many a barrier. Besides, Soup and I both knew that Miss Kelly and Miss Webster were friends.

"Over there."

Miss Webster pointed at an open dictionary cradled in a wooden rack on one of the reading tables.

Licking his thumb, Soup started flipping through the giant dictionary, turning each yellowing page with less care than its fragility demanded.

"Is it a dirty word?" I asked Soup.

"Don't be silly," Soup said. "Besides, I already *know* all the dirty ones. The word I'm looking up is a *beautiful* word. I just suspect it."

"What's the word?"

"Rapture."

"Huh?" I couldn't believe it. There stood Soup, one sneaker atop the other, looking up Juliet's last name. Maybe he had a fever, or was coming down with something. Like old age.

Soup said, "Ah! Here it is."

"What's it say, Soup?" I asked, seeing as his view was closer than mine.

"Rapture," read Soup, "a state or experience of being

swept away by overwhelming emotion. An expression or manifestation of ecstasy or passion."

I smiled. "It sounds dirty."

"Well, it isn't," said Soup. "Rapture is just about the most beautiful word in this whole darn dictionary."

Meanwhile, there wasn't a cat in the county that could creep up on a mouse more quietly than the way Miss Webster tiptoed around the library. She sure could have snatched a fancy living as a sneak thief. Suddenly there she was, standing behind us, peering over her rimless glasses at the open dictionary, her eyes flowing down the column of words that began with R-A-P.

I don't know exactly which word grabbed her attention, but it must have been a hot one. With a croaking gasp of alarm, to protect our innocent little minds from moral decay, she banged the dictionary closed.

BAM!

I surpressed the urge to whisper "Shh!" to Miss Webster, a term she often employed when Soup and I invaded her book-lined tomb. You had to give Miss Webster credit. The library was *her* turf, and she defended it with honor.

"Luther, I have a good mind to report your conduct, and Robert's, to Miss Kelly. And, to your parents."

We left the library. Over my shoulder, I stole a last look at Miss Webster, who was smiling. I was glad she was having herself some rapture.

"I told you it was dirty, Soup."

Soup answered back only one word: "Rapture."

His face bore the expression of a sick calf, and for a fleeting instant I expected Soup to do what Ally Tidwell did. But instead Soup just sort of half grinned.

Beyond the library, in the direction of the building where we were educated each Monday through Friday, there was a park. Benches, a water fountain that hardly ever was turned on, and plenty of tall elms and maples.

"Where we going, Soup?"

"You'll see. There's something I gotta do."

"Here in the park?"

"Yup. In a place where she'll be sure to see it."

Pulling a jackknife from the hip pocket of his knickers, Soup snapped open the longer of two slightly tarnished blades. Walking over to the largest tree in the park, Soup stopped, exploring the bark on all sides until he found a spot that was smoother than its rough and gray surroundings.

"What are you going to do, Soup?"

"Just you watch," said Soup, "because it's high time you learned a few matters."

I watched Soup carve a large curve, and then another, forming a heart about the size of a dinner plate. Then, inside the heart, the tip of his jackknife etched out a series of letters until at last his handicraft was complete.

It read: LWV loves JR.

"I want the world to know," said Soup, "that Luther Wesley Vinson loves Juliet Rapture."

19

"Well," I said, "I can't say for sure that the whole *world* will know, but it seems to me that every doggone soul in town will take notice."

"Okay with me," said Soup. "Ours is a reckless love."

Wiping the shreds of oak bark off the stained blade and onto his pants, Soup snapped the knife shut, dropping it back into the dark of his pocket.

"And," said Soup, "the Raptures have moved here to stay."

"How do *you* know?"

"Juliet told me, Rob. Her dad's got a job in the mill, and on Monday she starts school. With us."

"School's almost over."

"Yeah," said Soup. "Summer vacation is right around the corner."

"Maybe there'll be more parties. You know, like the kind we went to last night at the Bissell's."

Soup sighed. "Boy, that was the best party I ever went to. Little did I know that I was going to meet Juliet Rapture, and hear her voice call my number."

I wanted to tell Soup what an ugly number Juliet Rapture was, but then thought better of it. When a guy carves a gal's initials into an oak tree, inside a heart, and with a very dull jackknife, I don't guess he wants to listen to how horrible she looks.

"Red hair," said Soup. "There's just something extra special about a red head. Juliet sure is a beauty. Tell me true, Rob. Don't you think that Juliet Rapture is about the prettiest gal in the whole world?"

I sort of nodded. "Well," I honestly told Soup, "I admit that you don't see a gal every day that looks like Juliet Rapture."

And with her missing tooth in front, I silently thought, I bet she can really spit.

three

Monday morning came.

We were in school, and Miss Kelly again introduced our new student, Miss Juliet Rapture, to all of us. Juliet was assigned a seat next to Norma Jean Bissell. I was grateful she wasn't sitting near *me*, for it was obvious that Juliet hadn't blossomed an ounce prettier over the weekend.

Uglier, if anything.

Yet the adoring eyes of Luther Wesley Vinson, carver of initials and enthusiastic participant in kissing games, never left Juliet for an instant. Not even when Miss Kelly suggested that we pull out our geography books to continue our devoted pursuit of the whereabouts of Egypt.

"Golly," sighed Soup. He was smiling as he stole glances at Juliet Rapture.

And then I noticed something else.

Janice Riker was also smiling, at Soup. Janice was looking at Soup in that same dreamy way that my pal was gazing at Juliet Rapture. *Why?* Janice was known for hating *everybody*, especially boys. And that usually went double for either Soup or me—ever since the pair of us ganged up on her after school last fall, which happened only one second before Janice Riker knocked our heads together. My hair hurt for a week.

Outside, a car honked.

"She's here," said Miss Kelly, looking out the window that faced the dirt road in front of the schoolhouse.

We all recognized the car horn. It belonged to Miss Boland, the county nurse, and she was all dressed in white, like always. I didn't know whether Miss Boland was the world's largest woman, yet I'd never seen a bigger one. Very few men in town were as big as Miss Boland. And here she marched right into our schoolroom, carrying an object that was even bigger. To me it looked like a two-dimensional giant human figure, constructed out of thin plywood, attached to its own stand.

"Hi, troops," said Miss Boland, making her usual triumphant entrance. Miss Boland stood the figure up in the corner, turning it around so that we could eye it full view.

"I give up," said Miss Kelly. "Who is it?"

Whoever it was, Miss Boland's cardboard hero was near to seven feet tall and holding some sort of shiny musical instrument. He had black hair and a tiny waxed mustache.

"Folks," said Miss Boland with a wide smile, "I am pleased to present Mr. Farina, one of Italy's finest musicians, who happens to be touring Vermont this coming summer. I shouldn't have to remind *anyone*"— Miss Boland looked sternly at Miss Kelly, sort of in fun—"that Mr. Farina is a world-renowned master of the French horn."

"I thought you said he was from Italy," I said to Miss Boland. "Is he?"

"He *is*. But the instrument he so brilliantly plays is called a French horn."

"How come he's only got one hand?" Soup asked.

"Ah," said Miss Boland as she busily dusted off Mr. Farina's silhouette with her hanky. "An excellent question. And the answer is, that when you play the French horn, your left hand works the three valves, while your *right* hand . . . the one you can't see . . . is up inside the brass bell."

Soup yawned.

"I'm so excited," said Miss Boland. "Just think, a world-famous instrumentalist is actually coming here to vacation. I heard he was coming just yesterday."

25

"Where," asked Miss Kelly, "did you unearth that cardboard likeness of Mr. Farina?"

"Over the weekend," said Miss Boland, still polishing and dusting, "I drove down to Bennington to visit my cousin. Her husband manages the local concert hall, and *he* said, now that the recital was over, I could have Mr. Farina's cutout picture. Which," added Miss Boland, "I am generously donating to further the culture of your school."

"What," prompted Miss Kelly, "do we all have to say to Miss Boland for her gift to us?"

"Thank you, Miss Boland," we all dutifully chorused, even though I wanted a cardboard of Mr. Farina about as much as I wanted another navel.

"You're welcome, kids," said our nurse in white, slumping wearily into Miss Kelly's chair. "Wow, am I whacked. Couldn't sleep a wink all night, just thinking about Mr. Farina's coming to town."

"He certainly is *tall*," observed Miss Kelly.

Miss Boland added, "And handsome," almost as though her remark was intended for Miss Kelly's ears alone. To me, Mr. Farina looked about as handsome as Juliet Rapture.

"What did you say his first name is?"

Miss Boland blushed. "Romeo."

Raising her glasses, Miss Kelly repeated, "Romeo?"

"Yes. Isn't that . . . *exotic?*"

Miss Kelly nodded.

"A tall Italian," said Miss Boland, "named Romeo,

who plays the French horn. And he's actually coming to town."

"I can't wait," Soup said dryly into my ear, in a voice that was totally bored.

Miss Boland jumped to her feet. "And now," our county nurse announced, "I've saved the *best* news for last."

"There's *more?*" asked Miss Kelly.

"Decidedly," said Miss Boland. "I almost forgot what *else* I brought. Don't go away. It's out in the car."

"We won't," Miss Kelly assured her.

Quicker than you could say Romeo Farina, our county nurse vanished, then sped back into the room in a burst of white. And pink! By a coat hanger, she held a bright pink uniform trimmed in silver spangles. It sparkled like morning frost.

"I've decided," puffed Miss Boland, "that what this town needs is . . ."

"A pink circus uniform?" asked Miss Kelly.

"No," said Miss Boland.

"What then?"

"A band."

"Why this sudden interest in music?" Miss Kelly wanted to know. "As if I couldn't guess."

Miss Boland cleared her throat, trying not to look at the giant cutout of Mr. Farina. "I have *always* been a music fan. Have you forgotten that I used to toot a pretty sweet clarinet?"

"No one," said Miss Kelly, "could ever forget your

clarinet. In fact, only a few years ago, we could boast of quite a town band."

Miss Boland nodded one very firm nod. "Right. And I say we ought to revive it."

"When?"

"Sooner the better," said Miss Boland. "In fact, we don't have a moment to lose. Not one beat."

"But you can't form much of a band out of *one* uniform," said Miss Kelly, "and *one* clarinet."

Miss Boland's eyes widened. "That's just what I'm getting at. I went to the Grange Hall this morning and found our complete set of uniforms, all on hangers. Some a bit frayed or mussed, but little that couldn't be patched up. Each one pinker than a pig in love."

"How many?" asked Miss Kelly.

"Twenty or so."

"Well, twenty uniforms plus one clarinet still may sound a mite puny."

Miss Boland smiled. "It's a start."

From the corner of my eye, I saw Juliet Rapture raise her hand, a gesture immediately recognized by our teacher.

"Yes, Juliet?"

"Miss Kelly," said Juliet Rapture, "I can play a flute. Back where we used to live, I played in our junior band."

"Bless you," said Miss Boland. Then, turning to Miss Kelly, she added, "Amazing how once a band gets formed, it starts to grow."

"Indeed."

"All we need," said Miss Boland, "is eighteen more."

Soup raised his hand.

"Yes, Luther?"

"*I'll* be in the band, Miss Boland."

"Excellent. See? Here's one more."

"Hey," I whispered to Soup, "how can *you* be in the band? You don't know how to toot an instrument, do you?"

"Not yet," Soup whispered back. "But at the party last Friday I found out that I'm one heck of a quick learner."

Miss Kelly looked at Soup with a surprised expression. "Luther, you never told us of your musical interests."

"No," echoed Miss Boland. "What do you play?"

Soup coughed. "Well, it's sort of a surprise."

"It sure is," I whispered to Soup. "Even to you."

"Bully," said Miss Boland. "We've got a trio already and we haven't even begun. That means only seventeen more."

"My dad," said Norma Jean Bissell, "can play the saxaphone. But only in the key of G."

"Four!" chirped Miss Boland.

"And my Aunt Carol," said Wayne, "is still pretty good on the autoharp. Mama says she only attempts it when she gets tanked up."

As a warning to change the subject from beverages back to bands Miss Kelly cleared her throat.

"Five!" hooted Miss Boland.

"Anyone else?" asked Miss Kelly.

"My grandfather," said Rolly McGraw, "is still handy

with a tuba. But he's at least seventy-three, and maybe even older."

"Six!"

"Hmm," said Miss Kelly, "doesn't old Mr. Jubert who owns the candy store play a fiddle?"

"Sure does," said Ally Tidwell. "I hear tell Mr. Jubert plays for square dances over in Brandon every Friday night."

"Seven!"

"Say," said George Davis, "my Uncle Job got a ukulele for Christmas one year. I think he can play three chords."

"Hah!" snorted Miss Boland. "Eight."

"Perhaps," said Miss Kelly, "we could run a tiny advertisement in the weekly paper. I bet we could recruit enough players and instruments to fill all twenty of your pink uniforms."

"You're darn tootin'," said Miss Boland.

"Perhaps by Christmas," Miss Kelly said, "your band will be ready for its first recital."

"Bosh," said Miss Boland. "We'll be primed up *way* before that. So ready that we can make our debut on the Fourth of July."

"But that's only two weeks away."

"We'll just have to crank it up real fast."

Miss Boland held her mouth in a firm and determined pose. Our county nurse was hardly the type of person folks often say no to. If something could be done, Miss Boland could do it, even if it was to move the Fourth of July up to June.

30

"Now then," said Miss Boland, "we have a clarinet, a flute, a surprise from Luther here, saxophone, autoharp, tuba, fiddle, and ukulele. Say! My sister in Bennington plays the dulcimer."

"Nine," said Miss Kelly.

"Golly," said Miss Boland, "at the rate we're growing, we'll need *forty* uniforms instead of only twenty. We'll have to rent out the whole Grange Hall just to rehearse."

"Are you sure you can learn enough marches by the Fourth of July?" asked Miss Kelly.

Miss Boland froze. "*Marches?*"

"Of course," said Miss Kelly. "Fourth of July in this town amounts to just one thing."

"And what might that be?"

"Our big parade."

"That means," said Miss Boland, "that we'll have to master *marching* as well as music."

"You can do it," said Miss Kelly. "Don't you all agree, children?"

We responded with a hearty ovation, a declaration of confidence that gave Miss Boland renewed heart.

"Thank you, gang," she said.

"And," said Soup, "you'll have one *more* instrument, come summer. The one you forgot all about."

"Which one's that?"

Soup pointed at the cardboard figure of Mr. Romeo Farina. "A French horn."

four

"Come on, Rob."

"I'm coming," I told Soup.

My pal Soup was a bit more than a year older than I was. He was also taller and faster.

Today was Tuesday; and tomorrow, after school, the first band practice was to be held. This meant only one thing. If Soup and I were to become members of the band, we'd have to find ourselves a couple of musical instruments. And old Soup had said earlier that he knew where we'd best look.

Soup was yelling, "Let's go."

School was over for the day. Instead of heading for home, Soup had come up with the idea that if all the pink band uniforms were at the Grange Hall, then maybe a few extra instruments would be there too. He was a real planner.

"Wait up, Soup. I'm winded."

"Hurry up, slowpoke."

"Okay. I'm hurrying."

The front door of the Grange Hall was locked. It was an old building that was rarely used during the day, but in the evenings the hall was often filled with local farmers who came there to discuss produce prices. Sometimes, on a Saturday night, they'd hold a social or a dance. As the main hall contained stacks of folding chairs, the Grange would be an ideal place to hold a band practice. Or so Miss Boland said.

Sneaking around to the back, Soup helped me pry open a dusty window and slip inside, over the sash and its row of dead bugs. The auditorium was stuffy and airless.

Finding the band uniforms was no problem at all. There they were, neatly hung, where Miss Boland had said they'd be.

"Let's try one on," said Soup.

"Maybe we'd best not," I said. "We could get into trouble. You can put on a uniform if you want to, Soup. Not me."

"Why not?"

34

"Because . . . whenever you start suggesting something to do, it always means trouble, and I get caught."

"Here," said Soup.

He held up a silvery pink uniform that was exactly my size. It was beautiful. Mr. P. T. Barnum himself had never designed a band uniform as dazzling as the one that Soup was now carefully removing from its hanger.

"I won't do it."

"Nobody," said Soup, "says you gotta."

"Good."

"Maybe I'll do it," Soup said.

Almost as soon as he announced his intentions, Soup was wearing the beautiful pink jacket.

"Wow!" said Soup. "Do I ever feel like some sort of a nobleman or king or something."

"Honest?"

"Yup," said Soup. "But this jacket's a bit snug on me. It might probably fit you a size neater."

"Well," I said, "maybe so."

"Do you want to try it on?" Soup shed the pink jacket, holding it open so that I could slip into it.

Soup was right. It made me feel great. We even found a mirror behind a door, where I could look at myself.

Soup frowned. "Something's wrong," he said.

"Like what?"

"Well, to be truthful about it, you just don't look very dressy, that's all. Maybe it's because the pink jacket sort of outshines your faded old jeans."

35

"Yeah," I told Soup, "it sort of does."

"I'll fetch the pants," Soup offered.

A minute later, dressed in both pink trousers and pink jacket, plus a pink and silver cap, I stood looking at myself in the mirror. I was really beautiful. All I could think of was how much I wanted Norma Jean Bissell to see me. And right then, as if old Soup was reading my mind, he spoke out.

"Yup," said Soup, "you sure will impress Norma Jean in that pink getup. Maybe you ought to take a stroll over to her house and show her. One look and she'd kiss you from now until next Easter."

"I don't guess I ought to do that. Somebody might see me, Soup."

"Somebody like Norma Jean Bissell?"

"Yeah. That'd be real nifty."

"Say, I almost forgot," said Soup.

"Forgot what?"

"We'd best remember what we came here to do."

"Look for instruments."

"Right," said Soup.

We looked. Turning over barrels and peering into bales and dusty old boxes, we found spare parts for a milking machine, political leaflets left over from the Warren G. Harding presidential election, plus some pamphlets on the crop rotation of corn and alfalfa. But in the line of harmony we didn't uncover as much as a silent dog whistle.

36

Soup looked up at the ceiling. "Ah!"

"What is it, Soup?"

"See that pull rope, Rob?"

"Of course I see it."

"That," said Soup, "just might be the key to the top floor."

Standing on my pink, silvery, and uniformed shoulders, Soup reached the cord. And pulled. Down from the ceiling unfolded a zigzag of rickety stairs. Plus a hornet that seemed a bit upset that his dark domain, the Grange Hall attic, had been discovered.

"We're in luck," said Soup, just as the hornet stung my ear.

"*Yow!*"

Leaving me to battle the hornet, Soup scampered up the funny old stairway, complaining about the heat and also about the fact that he couldn't see a thing. I didn't care a whole lot, being as busy as I was with my own personal hornet.

Above my head, Soup tripped.

Boom! I heard a muffled sound, a booming I had heard somewhere before, but my ears couldn't quite recognize the noise. Maybe it was thunder.

From above, Soup's voice was an echo in the dark as he hollered out his next exclamation: "Eureka!"

"What is it, Soup?"

I was more interested now that I had finally managed to shoo away the hornet. My ear was still throbbing.

37

"Rob, I hit the jackpot."

"Like what?"

"It's in sort of a canvas cover, out of sight," said Soup. "But I can feel it. Yes! This is it! Couldn't possible be anything else. Not when it's *this* big."

Ear stinging, I carefully climbed the unfolded stairs that led to the hottest Grange Hall attic in forty-eight states.

"Careful," warned Soup.

"About what?"

"Well, if you walk on the wooden beams, you'll be okay, but if you step on the white squares of plaster you could fall yourself through."

"I'll be careful."

The attic was hotter than a band uniform. I stood there, itching inside the pink costume, waiting for my eyes to adjust to the darksome. Then I saw Soup, squatting near a very large object in the shape of a giant hockey puck.

"It's mine," said Soup. "I found it."

"Okay, it's yours. Whatever it is."

"Wow! I can't believe it, Rob."

"Neither can I. What in the deuce are we talking about?"

"This," said Soup, raising it up at an angle. Whipping back his foot, Soup kicked the big hockey puck, with force.

Boom!

"Hey!" I said. "It's a drum."

How the pair of us ever worked that enormous drum across the attic and down the rickety flight of stairs, I'll never know. Soup gave directions while I supplied most of the muscle, sweat, and bruises—and endured the irate attack of three more hornets. They must have been music lovers that knew what Soup and I were up to.

Bees, bugs, and hornets never seemed to sting Luther Wesley Vinson. Maybe because they'd worry that they might die of blood poisoning. I swatted, lugged, tugged, strained and pulled, hefted and huffed and heaved, until the drum was home free.

We closed the stairs. Up they went, to hide once more the steaming mysteries of the Grange Hall attic.

"Let's open her up," Soup said.

"Okay."

Unfastening snap after snap, Soup stripped off the canvas cover, and we saw the big bass drum for the first time. Standing up, it was taller than Soup. We read the letters on the drumhead: BIG BOY.

In smaller letters, we were informed that Big Boy was manufactured by the Dixie Dandy Drum Company of Valdosta, Georgia. Also, in a separate side pocket of the cover, we found a matched pair of woolheaded drumsticks. Each handle measured almost two feet in length, the tip of which fluffed out like a furry potato masher.

Slipping the harness straps around his shoulders, then

tightening the buckles, Soup tried to lift the drum. No dice. It was just too heavy.

"Big Boy," said Soup, "sure lives up to his name. This is one big instrument, this here drum of yours."

"*Mine?*"

Soup scratched his head. "Maybe if I help you carry it . . ."

"Me? Carry *that?*"

"Of course. You want to be in the parade on the Fourth of July, don't you?"

"Yes," I said. "But . . ."

"So," said Soup, "you want Norma Jean Bissell to see you in your pink uniform, I bet."

"Sure I do."

"Then I'll be a pal," said Soup. "I'll help you carry it. You march in front of the drum, where Norma Jean can see you as we march along Main Street, and I'll sort of hold up the rear. But *you're* the leader."

"You mean the drum's *mine?*"

"All *yours*," said Soup with a grin. "I'll tell Miss Boland how *you* found the drum. Not that we're stealing it or anything. We don't aim to keep it, or sell it."

"Only play it," I said.

"Right," said Soup. "You in front, me in back. Your job is the important one because it'll be up to you to steer. Like the captain on a ship. All I do is tag along and hold up the back end. You even get to wear the harness, while I carry the drum. And the sticks."

40

"Thanks a lot, Soup." I felt really happy. "You sure are a regular pal."

"Shucks," said Soup, trying not to laugh.

We left the drum in the Grange Hall and were halfway home when I became suddenly aware of something important. I was still dressed in pink.

five

"And so," said Miss Kelly, "we see on our maps of Europe that Italy is most easy to recognize."

We all had our geography books open to page 114 where there was a map of Europe in color.

"Italy," continued Miss Kelly, "is in the shape of a *what?*"

Janice Riker raised her hand. "A French horn."

Miss Kelly sighed.

Soup said, "It's a boot, Miss Kelly."

"Quite correct, Luther."

Soup smiled, yet it was nothing compared to the smile that Janice fired Soup's way. I hated it when Janice Riker smiled at *me*. It usually meant that she was going to get me after school, knock me flat, snake off my knickers and toss them into the bin of a passing pickup truck that had a full tank of gas and was headed out of town.

But I couldn't worry too much about why Janice Riker was smiling. All I could think about, instead of concentrating on the shape of Italy, was my drum. Well, actually it had earlier been Soup's drum. After all, Soup was the one who found it. But now that the drum was officially mine, according to Soup, I sure wasn't in the mood to argue a whole lot. *My* drum.

I could hardly wait for band practice.

"You see," said Miss Kelly, "as the Nile flows northward, it enters the Mediterranean in what is known as a delta, a fan-shaped area that is a vast deposit of silt. Now, who can tell us where *silt* comes from?"

Janice Riker again raised her hand. "Silt," she announced in her deep and rasping voice, "comes from a silt worm . . . in Japan."

Even before Miss Kelly could wince her reaction to Janice's brilliance, the toot of a familiar and welcome car horn heralded the arrival of Miss Boland. She was, as always, in her spotless white uniform and, as always, she was smiling.

"Greetings," said Miss Boland. She came in carrying

an oblong and black and very dusty case, which she opened up in order to withdraw a shiny silver object.

"Guys and gals," said Miss Boland, "how many of you know what I now hold in my hand?"

"A clarinet," said Juliet Rapture.

Turning around, Soup smiled at her freckled face, and I thought he seemed prouder than if *he* had answered Miss Boland's question.

"Brains as well as beauty," whispered Soup.

Miss Boland was busily sucking at what looked like one of her tongue depressors, the kind she used to poke at a sore throat. It was shorter and more narrow than a depressor, but the same pale color.

"This," said Miss Boland, "is a reed. Without it, a clarinet would sound absolutely dreadful."

Installing the reed in the mouthpiece, Miss Boland limbered her chubby fingers, lifted her clarinet to her lips, and played what once might have been "Juanita." The noise she manufactured could never rightfully have been termed music. It sounded halfway between a sawmill and a goose honk, from a goose whose throat should have been examined with one of those little tongue depressors. When your fingernail scrapes down the blackboard, it sounds much like Miss Boland's silver clarinet. "Juanita" sure needed an oiling.

But I'll say this for Miss Kelly. She stood her ground, even forcing a smile with every sour squawking screech and scream that our county nurse's instrument wailed out. The clarinet was no doubt being bitten on the reed by Miss Boland, and was gasping in torment.

Finally she quit. "Guess I'm a bit rusty," she said, "but I'll be warmed up by this afternoon. Practice at three o'clock. Everybody *be* there. That is, everyone who, like myself, has a musical inclination."

Miss Kelly smiled.

"And," said Miss Boland, "we have a few extra instruments for those who fail to bring their own."

"Like what, Miss Boland?"

"Oh, let's see. We have a triangle, a snare drum, castanets, a pair of brass cymbals, and a glockenspiel. All you do is hit a lyre with a hammer."

I always knew that I got punished whenever I told a fib, but I sure had no idea that a liar in a band got hammered. Maybe all this band business was more serious than I thought.

"Okay," said Miss Boland. "By a silent show of raised hands, how many of you plan to come to band practice today?"

Only three hands went up. In this order: Juliet Rapture's, Soup's, and my own.

"Humpf!" snorted Miss Boland. "Well then, if *that's* the kind of say-die spirit, maybe we won't have a band at all."

As she spoke, Miss Boland looked rather longingly at the giant plywood likeness of Mr. Romeo Farina and his French horn. Yet, knowing Miss Boland as I did, I figured she was a long shot away from throwing in the towel.

I was right. Miss Boland fired a sly wink at Miss Kelly, who smiled back at her friend.

"Kids," said Miss Boland, "have you ever heard of a company called Super-Sweet Fireworks?"

Our eyes widened. There wasn't a solitary kid in America who hadn't spent his lifelong earnings during the first three days of every July in order to stock his arsenal with cherry bombs, sizzlers, firecones, sparklers, roman candles, skyrockets, pinwheels, and firecrackers galore . . . all proud products of the Super-Sweet Fireworks Company.

Many a finger had been scorched, as well as an eardrum shattered, by the Fourth of July temptations packaged by the careless hands of Super-Sweet Fireworks. Yet there wasn't a child in all of Vermont unwilling to risk permanent injury in order to inhale the ignited sulfur and saltpeter fumes of such explosive treasures.

"Well," said Miss Boland, reading the look of dedicated awe on our faces, "I just *might* be able to get a friend of mine, who works for the company, to stop his truck right here in town and put on the biggest Fourth of July fireworks show that this community will ever witness. For *free*."

Wow! I was too excited even to breathe.

"But," warned Miss Boland, "I surely couldn't ask this

friend of mine to visit a town that didn't have a band, could I?"

"No," we all sighed.

"I do believe," said Miss Kelly, "that what Miss Boland is offering is a swap. If you join the new marching band, you'll be rewarded by being allowed to watch an outstanding display of fireworks. Am I correct, Miss Boland?"

"Absolutely," said Miss Boland with one of her absolute nods of her white nurse's cap. "No band, no fireworks."

"Fair enough," added Miss Kelly.

"Now then," said Miss Boland, "band practice is at the old Grange Hall at three o'clock. We'll learn the music today, and as for the marching in step and in formation, we'll tackle that tomorrow."

This sure is fun, I thought. And it'll be the most colorful, star-studded Fourth of July we've ever held. I could hardly wait. Closing my eyes, I was once again dressed up in my handsome pink uniform, carrying Soup's drum. No! Carrying *my* drum. After all, Soup had said it was now *mine*.

It was odd. Rarely was old Soup as generous as all that. Yet he had volunteered to carry the drum and march in back of it while I was up front, the leader. Gee!

Miss Boland left, waving so long to us all, and firing farewell reminders to us to report to the Grange Hall right after recess.

We continued our study of Italy, under the guidance of Miss Kelly, who touched on the fact that Mr. Romeo Farina, the famous Italian, would soon be among us. And with luck perhaps we could persuade him to become, for the duration of his stay in our vicinity, a full-fledged member of the new town band.

Miss Kelly's suggestion was met with unanimous approval, especially from those of us who fervently hoped that a French horn could help drown out the screeches of a certain clarinet.

Soup continued to sigh deep sighs, staring at Juliet Rapture while Janice did likewise in Soup's direction. Something funny was going on. But I sure wasn't in on it. It worried me so much that I couldn't even concentrate on staring at Norma Jean Bissell. My thoughts wandered. So badly, that on several occasions, I caught myself actually thinking about Italy and Egypt.

Such was my early afternoon.

Finally, it came: Miss Kelly rang the recess bell. We lined up in a row in order to shake hands with our teacher and explode into what remained of a day's freedom from the burdens of scholarship. Kids ran for home.

Then, outside the school, it happened. Janice jumped Soup.

I knew something weird was going to happen. I felt it in my bones. And it certain enough did. Soup didn't have a chance. Down he went with Janice on top, as usual.

49

I was panicky. Not knowing what to do, I sort of ran back and forth between where Janice held Soup and where I might solicit emergency aid from Miss Kelly. If I acted in time, I might be able to prevent Soup's getting too badly damaged.

I couldn't believe what I saw. Soup was down. Janice was on top of him, her big old knees pinning the muscles of his upper arms. My pal was a goner, completely helpless. Any second, I knew that Janice's fist, armed with all forty-three knuckles and harder than a railroad spike, would be crashing into poor Soup's defenseless jaw.

"Help!" yelled Soup. "Rob!"

Then it happened. Janice didn't punch, or kick, or even bite. It was far worse than that. Never did I realize that Janice Riker was capable of inflicting such an indignity on a schoolmate.

She kissed Soup.

Again and again, all over his yelping face, Janice planted her power-packed puckering smooches. "I love you too, Luther," said Janice.

"Huh?" said Soup.

"I saw it," purred Janice, "and it sure was a sweet surprise, Luther."

Watching in horror, my feet felt frozen to the dirt. I couldn't even force myself to help defend my comrade. And no words could I think of that would make Janice relent from her attack on poor unfortunate Soup.

"The tree," Janice said to Soup. "I couldn't wait to

thank you, Luther." She kissed him again, smothering his plaintive yells for help.

Then I looked over at that big old tree where Soup had so recently carved *LWV loves JR.*

J.R. . . . Janice Riker?

SIX

"Places," ordered Miss Boland.

We were all standing in the Grange Hall, about eighteen people—half of them adults and half kids. Soup and I had gotten there early to help Miss Boland set up the folding chairs in semicircular rows.

"Mr. Jubert," said Miss Boland to the tall and lean proprietor of the town's only candy store, "would you please sit in the front row, up here, right next to Mr. Petty."

"No," said Mr. Jubert, "I won't."

"Why not?" asked Miss Boland. "Is it the front row that you object to?"

Mr. Horrace Jubert snorted, holding his fiddle under his chin as he tightened a string. "I refuse to sit next to a trombone."

"But," said Miss Boland, "your violin and Mr. Petty's slide trombone will sound good together."

Mr. Petty blew a sour note on his trombone, with its spit valve open, as if to say that he had no intention of sitting anywhere in the same *county* with Mr. Jubert.

"I happen," said Mr. Jubert, "to *hate* the sound of a trombone, and I don't guess I ever liked anyone who plays one."

"That," said Mr. Edgar Petty, our local barber, "goes double for me. A trombone happens to be a *cultural* instrument, which is more than I can say for fiddle scratching."

"Where will I sit?" asked a new voice.

Soup and I turned to notice Aunt Carol, Wayne's aunt. She was holding her autoharp, an instrument that appeared as if it had been the sole survivor of the Battle of Bull Run.

"Well," said Miss Boland, "it really doesn't make a whale of a difference where *anyone* sits."

"How come?"

"Because, on the Fourth of July, we're not going to be sitting. We'll be in the parade, *marching*."

"That being the case," said Mr. Jubert, "I also won't *march* with a trombone."

54

"And I won't walk a single solitary step," said Mr. Petty, "unless you put the fiddlers in the back row where they belong."

Miss Boland then announced that *she* would sit between Mr. Jubert and Mr. Petty, in spite of Mr. Jubert's allowing that he also disliked clarinets . . . And females.

"Where does the ukulele sit?"

"Ah," said Miss Boland, "how about next to the big drum?"

"But," said Soup, "you said the *flute* could be here."

I could tell that what Soup yearned for was not a flute but a flutist, Miss Juliet Rapture. She finally arrived.

"Okay," said Miss Boland, "I give up. You can all sit wherever you choose, seeing as this is only a rehearsal."

The door opened. In came the town's oldest citizen, Mr. Dumas Mack, wearing his Spanish-American War uniform and waving his U.S. Army bugle. "I'm here," he hooted, limping forward to join our group of musicians.

"We don't need a bugle in a band," I heard Mr. Petty remark to Mrs. Furdock.

"Why not?"

"They're bad luck."

"I never heard *that* before."

"Well," said Mr. Petty, "they certain are. It was back in 1903 when they all formed a band up in Hodge Corners, and they made the fatal mistake of allowing a bugler to join up."

"What happened?"

"I forget," said Mr. Petty. "I just heard it said that a bugle can mean nothing but bad luck to a band. Sort of like a curse you get when a black cow crosses your path."

"You mean a black *cat*."

"Same thing. You should never tempt the fates, I say, and let a cow join a band. Or rather a bugle."

Several citizens of varied shapes and ages stood idle. They were quickly assigned instruments by Miss Boland. Then, as we were just about to get under way and attack some music, Mrs. Stetson entered via the back door.

"I'm here," she firmly announced.

"Good," said Miss Boland. "What do you play?"

Raising her eyebrows, Mrs. Stetson said, "I don't play anything. I *sing*."

"We don't need a vocalist," said Mr. Jubert. "This isn't a church choir. It's a band."

"*Someone* has to sing," said Mrs. Stetson, "and I have sung every Sunday morning in the Baptist church for over thirty years."

"Over sixty would be closer," said Mr. Petty.

"I heard," said Mrs. Stetson, "that *everyone* would be welcome."

"Except," said Mr. Petty, "for singers and buglers."

"And trombones," added Mr. Jubert.

"Naturally," said Miss Boland, "you certainly are welcome to join, just in case we play 'The Star Spangled Banner.' "

"Let's play *something*," said Mr. Jubert. "This dang

wooden chair is about to kill my rump. I say we all ought to play standing up."

"Can't," said Aunt Carol.

"Why not?"

"It's the corn I'm nursing on my big toe. You folks don't know what misery is until you suffer a corn."

"Huh," said Mr. Petty. "It can't be any worse than water on the knee."

"Since when have you had *that*?"

"Never, thank Providence," said Mr. Petty. "But I heard tell it was a real tribulation."

"Very well," said Miss Boland, holding her clarinet high in the air like a baton, "when I bring my arms down, like *this*, it means we start playing. Okay?"

Everyone agreed.

Up went Miss Boland's clarinet once more. Down it came, yet no music was heard, except for Soup's one thump on Big Boy. Along with mine. The huge drum was resting on the floor between us. Yet it was still taller than both of us.

"Short number," said Mr. Jubert.

"You forgot," said Mr. Petty, "to tell us what song we were supposed to play."

Correcting her error, Miss Boland quickly handed out small booklets of sheet music to each band member. We, at last, were armed for our attack.

"Let's see," said Miss Boland, "what'll we play first?"

Mr. Petty said, "I like number thirteen."

"Which one is that?"

" 'When the Roll is Called Up Yonder, I'll be There.' "

"I don't like it," said Mr. Jubert.

"Well, I do," said Mrs. Stetson. "It's a lovely old hymn. And I've sung it many times in the choir. In fact, I could sing the words right now . . ."

"Perhaps," said Miss Boland, "we'll start with something else. A real rouser. Some piece that's got plenty of pep."

Somebody suggested "Over There," a march that everyone seemed to agree was high-spirited enough for an opener. The only trouble was, the music for "Over There" was not in our booklets.

Mr. Petty suggested, seeing as we were leading up to the Fourth of July, that we'd best stick to music that was patriotic.

Mrs. Stetson said that she could also sing almost three verses of "Indian Love Call."

"Nope," hollered Dumas Mack, who talked as if everyone *else* was deaf.

"Why not?"

"Because if there's one song that's near impossible to play on a bugle, it's 'Deep Purple.' "

Miss Boland sighed.

"If you ask me," said Mr. Jubert, "we might consider doing an old square dance tune."

"Like what?"

"Well, like 'Honolulu Baby.' "

"No, ya don't," said Mr. Petty. "All you care about is that dangfool fiddle and all that hillybilly stuff you play."

58

"I don't either. I'll compromise for the sake of harmony."

"So will I."

"Good," said Aunt Carol, "because I have yet to speak up with *my* suggestion."

"Which is?"

"I think we ought to do a South American number. After all, we *do* have castanets. So I say we try 'Lady of Spain, I Adore You.'"

"Spain's not in South America," said Soup.

"Dang them Spaniards," said Dumas Mack, who then raised his bugle to his aging lips and blew a bugle call we all recognized as "Charge." Mr. Mack, as everyone knew, had been a bugler in the Spanish-American War.

When he was done, Mrs. Stetson remarked that the bugle rang very patriotic to *her* ear, and that we should consider starting the parade with "Taps."

"Hey," said Mr. Jubert, "look at number thirty-four."

"It's *missing* in my book. What is it?"

"'Whispering Hope.'"

"I know *every* verse," said Mrs. Stetson, "by heart."

"Huh," snorted Mr. Petty. "You sure as heck didn't remember all the words when you sang it in church last Easter. For close to an entire stanza, we all witnessed you standing there with your mouth open, and not one note coming out."

"That," said Mrs. Stetson, "was because a bug flew in my mouth. I think it was a moth miller."

"Last winter," said Aunt Carol, "we had the worst time

with moth millers. Any year you have a warm autumn, look out, because you'll have a moth in every pocket. And nothing gets rid of 'em once they nest and start breeding."

"I heard," said Mr. Petty, "that if you dip your clothes in buttermilk, you won't have millers at all. Just roaches."

"That's a fact," agreed Mrs. Stetson. "That's why I stopped buttermilking my clothes. I only do the blankets. The secret is, right after, you got to rinse the buttermilk out with vinegar. Cuts the curds."

"Epsom salts works better. I use it every fall when I get out my good purple dress."

"I still like 'Deep Purple.' So does everyone else. A real crowd-pleaser. It'd be a sure-fire hit, because anybody who calls himself a music lover likes 'Deep Purple.'"

"I don't," yelled old Mr. Mack. "If you want my opinion, we could start the parade real proper with 'Boots and Saddles.'"

"Say," said Mr. Petty, "I saw a cowboy movie one time where this calvalry bugler was sounding his horn, and an injun arrow killed his horse."

"Let's play 'Indian Love Call.'"

Right then I heard a stomach growl.

"I'm getting hungry," said Mr. Jubert. "Either we play *something*—or I'm going home to supper."

"Hold it, please," Miss Boland pleaded. "We can't break up our practice until we play at least *one* song. Are there any more suggestions?"

" 'Little Sir Echo.' "

" 'Battle Hymn of the Republic.' "

"Number eighteen."

"What is that?"

"I don't know. All I can see is the notes. The title got torn off the paper. But it's in the key of G."

"Something spiritual," said Mrs. Stetson.

"Anything but square dance music," said Mr. Petty, glowering at Mr. Jubert's fiddle.

"How about 'Song of India'?"

" 'Twelfth Street Rag.' "

" 'Mother Macree.' "

" 'Stars and Stripes Forever.' "

" 'They Call Him Mr. Touchdown.' "

"Wow," said Soup, "we sure know the names of lots of songs."

"Yeah," I said. "It's hard to believe we'd get so good in just the first practice."

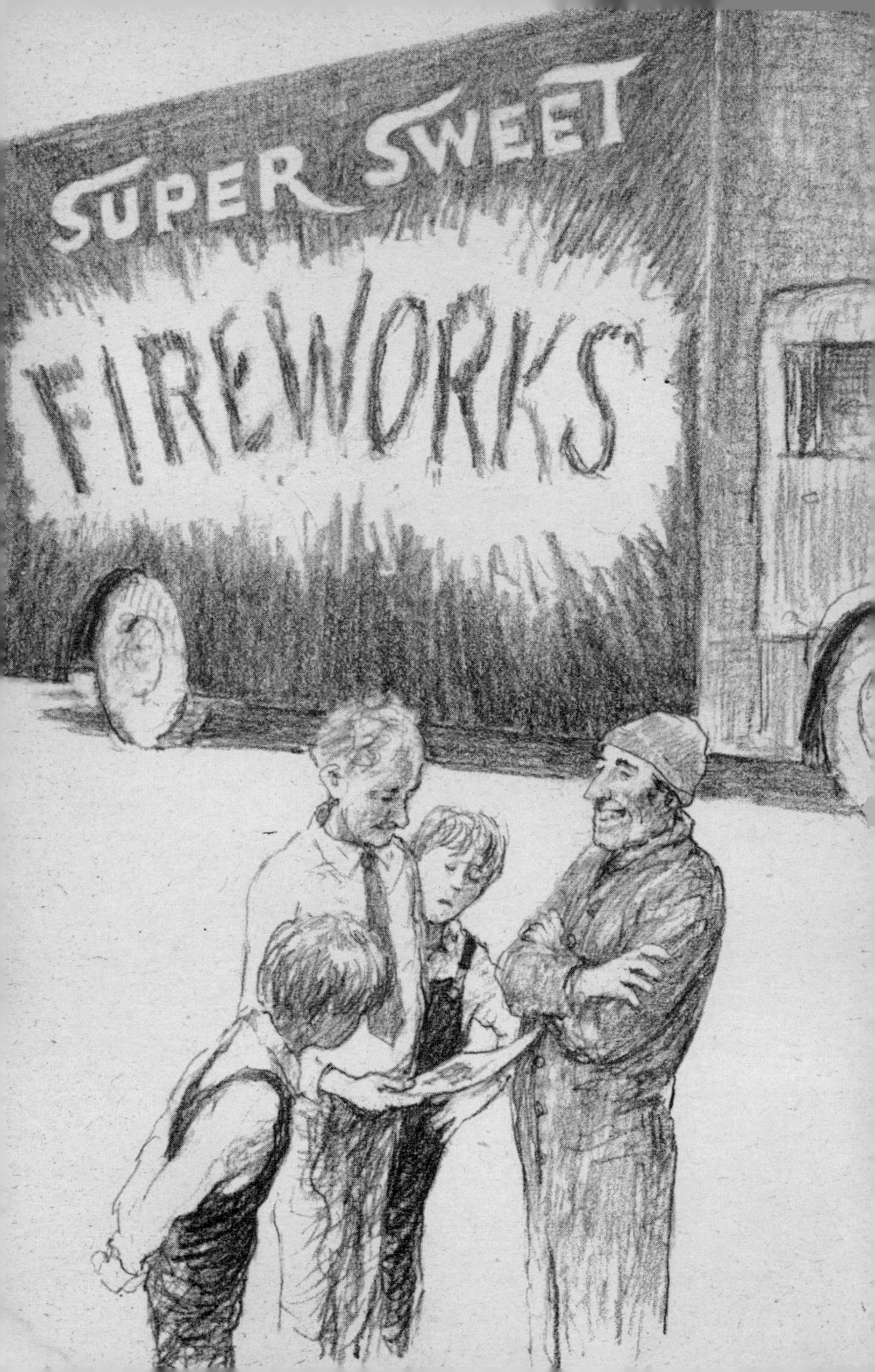
SUPER SWEET
FIREWORKS

seven

"It's here!" hollered Soup.

Looking out our kitchen window, I saw Soup running down the west meadow that separated the Vinson's farm from ours. With a dish towel over my shoulder, I was standing at our kitchen sink helping Aunt Carrie finish up the breakfast dishes.

"Hey!" I yelled out the open window, making Aunt Carrie drop a coffee mug back into a sudsy dishpan. "What's here?"

"The truck. The truck's in town."

Out of breath, Soup stormed into the kitchen, banging the screen door. Aunt Carrie shut her eyes and, for once, said nothing at all as Soup collapsed into a chair at the kitchen table.

"What truck?" asked Aunt Carrie. The silence was too much for her.

"The Super-Sweet Fireworks truck," said Soup.

"How do *you* know?"

"Because old Ben Turley just stopped by our place on his way up road, and told Pa. I asked him if I could skip into town and see it."

"What'd he say?"

Soup looked at Aunt Carrie. "He said okay, long as I got myself home by chore time."

"Fireworks," snorted Aunt Carrie, who over the years had shown little fondness for loud noises—including Soup.

"Yes'm," said Soup. "Today's the day that they're going to put up all the fancy fireworks for the Fourth of July."

"Where?"

"Over in the baseball park," said Soup. "I guess that's about the most open place they could find that's anywhere near the center of town."

Aunt Carrie looked squarely at me, her red hands

dripping with soap bubbles. "You're not going."

My heart sank.

But then Mama came downstairs and into the kitchen. "Where isn't he going?"

"Well," said Aunt Carrie, "if you ask me, I don't guess there's one sane reason why two half-growed boys have to scoot into town just to greet a tomfool truckful of firecrackers."

"Who said fireworks were in town?"

"Ben Turley," said Aunt Carrie. "And he's never got one thing straight in his entire life. He'd hitch a mule behind a wagon."

"It's Saturday, Mama," I said.

"Let's go see," said Soup.

"Ought to be against the law," said Aunt Carrie. "Some folks in town won't be happy until they either blow up or burn down."

"The truck's in town," said Soup.

"My," said Mama, "seems like a century since we've had a real bang-up display for the Fourth of July."

Aunt Carrie thumped the empty dishpan. "I smell trouble." She looked at Soup as she spoke.

Soup glanced at my mother. "Pa said I could go into town and watch 'em unload the truck at the ballpark. Can Rob come?"

"Who's in charge?"

"I heard it was Rankin Delaney," said Soup. "He's the chairman of the Fourth of July committee, according to Miss Boland. So I guess he's to supervise the unloading."

"If you want my opinion," said Aunt Carrie, "I've seen Rank Delaney on many a Saturday, an he's never been *un*loaded!"

Mama laughed.

"We'll be careful," I said.

My mother sighed. "If we *do* let you two go to the ballpark, *will* you be careful and not touch any of the fireworks?"

"Yes'm," said Soup. "We'll be more careful than a porcupine in love."

Aunt Carrie gasped. But my mother turned her face toward the north window so that nobody could see she was chuckling.

"And you'll come back by noon?"

"Sure," lied Soup.

"Then you'd both best get started."

Banging the screen door, Soup and I charged from the kitchen, heading for town. It was more than a mile, but we made the ballpark in about ten minutes flat. Sure enough, just as Soup had predicted, there was the biggest truck I'd ever seen in my entire life.

"Wow!" said Soup.

The enormous truck was painted a flaming red, with an orange and yellow name on each side that seemed to explode its letters, just like the Fourth of July. It read SUPER-SWEET FIREWORKS.

"That," said Soup, "is what I call a truck."

I nodded. "Boy," I told Soup, "if I ever get growed up,

and buy a truck, it's going to look exactly like that one."

We saw Mr. Rankin Delaney talking to a man who was dressed in bright red coveralls, on the back of which was lettered SUPER-SWEET FIREWORKS.

"Now then," said Rank Delaney, "I reckon we can have the rockets all go up from somewhere just outside third base. Maybe out in left field."

"Okay," said the Super-Sweet guy.

"Which means," continued Mr. Delaney, "we can plant the boomer bombs over in right field, out of harm's way."

"Yep. That's fine and dandy."

"As I see it," said Mr. Delaney, "this leaves most all of center field for the lettering. Right?"

The fireworks man nodded. "Check."

"We want that for the grand finale," said Mr. Delaney. "Bombs first, just to attract everybody's attention. Then the sky rockets."

The man sighed. "Fine."

"And then the big finish. The grand finale. All the lettering spelled out across center field in red, white, and blue."

"Yup . . . sort of."

"What did you say it would read?"

"The usual. It'll say . . . here's a picture of it."

Soup and I crowded in close, on either side of Mr. Delaney, so we could all take a squint at the picture he was looking at. The burning letters read:

I LOVE A SUPER-SWEET FOURTH OF JULY.

"Gee," said Mr. Delaney, "that'll be great. But maybe we could just set it up to read 'Happy Fourth of July' if we run out of room."

"Nope," said the man.

"Why not?"

"Because the company's donating the fireworks this time around, for free. So we naturally want some advertising, too. Get it?"

"Yeah," said Mr. Delaney. "I reckon if we're getting all these doodads on the cuff, I s'pose we can put up with whatever ya got."

"Red, white, blue, purple, and gold," said the Super-Sweet Fireworks driver. "Miss Boland's a friend of my sister-in-law's, and she said that anything we donate would be okay with the town."

"Sometimes," said Rank Delaney, "that county nurse of ours makes too many decisions around here."

"Like what?"

"Well," said Mr. Delaney, "it's about the parade."

"We're going to be *in* it," said Soup.

"Who said?"

"Miss Boland," I said quickly. "Soup and I are part of the new marching band. And she said we'd be the first group to parade down Main Street on the Fourth of July."

Mr. Delaney snorted. "Well, it wasn't that way *last* summer. The Home Guard was first, because *we're* the ones with a color guard. You know, carrying the American flag. And *we always* lead the parade."

"We got pink uniforms," said Soup.

"Maybe so," said Mr. Delaney. "But don't forget the importance of the Home Guard as a military unit. Some of our members are veterans of the world war, and *we're* in uniform, too."

Mr. Petty, the barber, joined the conversation. "If you ask me," he said, "the band ought to march in *front* of the Home Guard. The band first, then the Boy Scouts and the Girl Scouts. After that, the new fire truck."

"You mean," said Mr. Delaney, "you'd put the Home Guard *behind* a fire truck?"

"Doggone right I would."

"That's not partiotic."

"Civic pride," said Mr. Petty, "is just as important as the Home Guard. Besides, you fellows are always out of step, because of Wheeler."

"Now look here, Petty. I'll have you know that Wheeler Powell happens to be my wife's cousin."

"Don't matter. He marches like he was home in his cow pasture, stepping over . . . things."

"He does not."

"Does so."

"No, he just *walks* a mite strange, that's all. You can't blame Wheeler if he's got a couple of trick knees."

"Yeah, and each one of his trick knees buckles up so high that every step he takes he darn near kicks himself in the chin."

"That's why Wheeler has to look straight up in the air when he walks."

"And every other step, he trips."

"Not always. It'll be different this year."

"How so?" asked Mr. Petty.

"Because this year," answered Mr. Delaney, "we thought we'd let Wheeler carry the flag."

"Why?"

"Well, to take his mind off his knees. Chin high, he'll be looking up at the flag and won't feel as if the bystanders are all staring at him."

"Nobody," said Mr. Petty, "would look at Wheeler Powell if there was anything else to look at."

"I s'pose you mean that lousy band."

"So happens, I mean just that. There's only one thing that's proper to lead a parade with, if you ask me," said Mr. Petty.

"And what's that?"

"A shiny, silvery slide trombone."

Mr. Delaney's face turned a shade more scarlet as he pointed a chubby finger at Mr. Edgar Petty. "Ha! That's a caution."

"It is, eh?"

"Only reason you claim a trombone ought to lead a parade is because *you* try to play one."

"What's that supposed to mean, *try?*"

"You heard me. No wonder the old town band broke up, years back, on account nobody could stand to listen to your goshawful slushpump."

"Don't you call my trombone a slushpump," Mr. Petty warned.

"You don't belong in a parade. You and that trombone ought to hire out to flush a septic tank."

"*Please*," said the fireworks man, "won't *somebody* help me unload this stuff?"

eight

"What's tomorrow?" asked Miss Kelly.

Smiling, we sat behind our desks. "The last day of school," we rapturously responded.

"Are you happy, too, Miss Kelly?" asked Soup.

"Of course I am. Yet, as each school year folds to a close, I know how empty summertime can be without all of you." She looked at each one of us in turn.

"Honest?"

Miss Kelly nodded. "At the end of every June, I feel more like late November, like a barren old maple tree that has shed her leaves and lost all her October tresses of red and gold. I'm an old maid, you see, and you children are my only family. And you keep me young, as you all are my green and growing garden."

The way Miss Kelly said it made me swallow. I sort of hoped that Soup didn't notice that I'd started to blink my eyes a little faster.

"Oh, how my garden grows," she said. "And for those of you who will leave us and attend the big central school next fall, I hope that you'll always hold happy memories, as will I."

"We will."

"Indeed you shall. I'm most fortunate to have grown such a glorious flowerbed, season upon season. And lived long enough to see so many of you ripen, and prosper, then blossom with a garden of your own."

"Like my folks," said Wayne.

Miss Kelly nodded. "Your mother and father both sat at these very desks, a long time ago. It was soon after I'd just begun to teach. Back in the days when I was also green."

As she spoke, Miss Kelly's hand reached up to touch her white hair. I wanted to touch her, too, sort of the way you'd pet a new calf.

"This school"—Miss Kelly lifted her eyes to the bare wooden rafter—"was a bit newer then, with a fresh coat

74

of white paint. I was equally fresh, I suppose. Fresh ideas, along with a pocketful of dreams."

"What was it like, Miss Kelly, back in olden times when you were young?"

Miss Kelly threw back her head, laughing so abruptly that her pencil fell out of her hair. "About the same as today," she said.

"Really?"

"Of course. Children behaved then as they do today. And my ruler was just as hard. If you doubt me, Wayne, ask your father."

"He remembers, Miss Kelly. He sure does."

"Yes, I know he remembers. Even now, he calls me Miss Kelly as though he were still my student."

"Miss Kelly," I asked her, "will you still be teaching when we have kids?"

She smiled. "Mercy, no! I should hope by then that we'll not only have ourselves a new elementary school, but to match, a fresh new face for a teacher."

"No," said Soup.

I sort of looked at Soup in surprise.

"We don't want a new teacher," said Soup. "We'll always want you, Miss Kelly."

Soup's face sort of colored up after he spoke up, but I knew he was glad he said what he did. I was glad, too. I didn't even like to walk by our old schoolhouse in the summertime or look at it, knowing that there wasn't any Miss Kelly inside. It always made my heart feel emptier than the school. Like my heart was haunted.

"Well," said Miss Kelly, "some September, not too many years from now, you'll all come trudging back to school . . . all you girls with shiny new ribbons tied to your pigtails, and you boys all smelling of a fresh haircut . . . and you'll find a new young face here, awaiting you."

We couldn't speak.

"And on that day," said Miss Kelly, "I want you to honor a favor I shall ask of you. It is my wish that you welcome your new teacher as warmly as you can, for you shall be teaching *her* as much, if not more, than she shall teach you."

The room was very quiet. Miss Kelly sat on the edge of her desk, hands folded in her lap, with fingers entwined. From the pocket of her dress she suddenly produced a small lace hanky, not bringing it up to her face but, with her fingers, squeezing it very hard. Her knuckles looked whiter than her hair.

I'd heard talk in town, among some grown ups, that maybe Miss Kelly ought to retire. They said she was old-fashioned. All I knew, as I sat behind my desk that morning, was that I wanted Miss Kelly to be at our school forever. *I love you.* Those were the words I never had the gumption to say to either Miss Kelly or Norma Jean Bissell. Yet those three words were beating inside my chest as I looked at my teacher.

Maybe, I thought, I'll save up for a jackknife, like Soup's. And right into the bark of that big tree, I'll carve a heart that will hold the words *Rob loves Miss Kelly*.

"How comforting a thought," Miss Kelly was saying, "at the end of each school year to review in our minds how much we have learned."

I wasn't quite sure I'd mastered Egypt yet, but I'd be doggoned if I was going to admit it. At least I knew it was in Africa, somewhere south of Europe. Anyhow, it sure was a far piece away from Vermont. I reckon I wasn't about to visit Cairo when I hadn't even been to Burlington yet.

A car honked.

Soup nudged me. "It sounds like Miss Boland."

"Yeah," I said, "it certain does."

"Rob," said Soup, "I never thought the day would come that I preference to get a needle in the arm from Miss Boland rather than hear her clarinet."

In she stormed. Miss Boland didn't really *enter* a room. She sort of *invaded* it.

"Gosh," whispered Soup.

What we saw was not our usual county nurse in a white uniform that looked bigger than a January mountain. Miss Boland wasn't in white. She was sort of in flowers. A walking greenhouse.

Miss Kelly blinked. "My stars."

Turning around in a full circle, Miss Boland said, "It's my new dress from Sears and Roebuck, and thank the goodness they sent it a size too big. It just fits."

Miss Boland's new dress sure was colorful. It sort of looked as if somebody had dynamited a paint factory. You couldn't name one single color of the rainbow that was missing. Daisies, butterflies, tulips . . . a pink lion on her shoulder and a purple tiger on her hip.

I fought my laughter and then lost, right after Soup made his remark: "She looks like a zoo on fire."

Come to think of it, I can't recall ever seeing Miss Boland in anything except her usual white nurse's dress. But today she was one powerful picture of pigment, sporting colors I never knew existed.

"Well," asked Miss Boland, "*say* something."

Miss Kelly swallowed. "Now *that*," she said to our nurse, "is what I'd really call an outstanding dress."

Miss Boland smiled. "I just had to slip into it."

Soup whispered into my ear. "To me, it looks more like she slipped *on* it."

"It's for Wednesday," said Miss Boland.

Miss Kelly's eyebrows raised. "Wednesday?"

I was a bit confused myself, as I already knew that Miss Kelly owned what she called her Sunday dress, which she wore on Parents Day, when we had to recite. It was navy blue with white lace on the collar and cuffs. But I had to confess that Miss Kelly's Sunday couldn't begin to match whatever it was that Miss Boland was planning for Wednesday. With such a colorful explosion of cloth, it just had to be that somebody was blowing up the world.

"You don't think it's too short?" asked Miss Boland.

Miss Kelly shook her head. "No, of course not. Times are changing. Best you keep yourself in style."

"The catalog said it's an *Italian* print."

"Italian?"

Miss Boland beamed a grin. "For this coming Wednesday."

"I can't stand the suspense," said Miss Kelly. "Tell us about Wednesday before we all expire from curiousity."

"It's the train," said Miss Boland. "On Wednesday afternoon, the train gets here."

Miss Kelly nodded her head very slowly, as though she'd spotted daylight. But I just looked at Soup and he looked at me.

"Rob," whispered Soup, "if anything could flag down The Green Mountain Limited, it's gotta be that dress."

"Either that," I muttered back, "or the poor engineer'll be so scared he'll throw the throttle so wide open that the train won't stop much short of the Arctic Circle."

"Guess," said Miss Boland "*who* is arriving in town, by train, this coming Wednesday?"

"Babe Ruth?" asked Janice Riker.

"No," said Miss Boland. "Guess again."

"Can you give us a hint?"

"Well," said Miss Boland, "he's very famous, not to mention quite tall, and he's from Italy. And he plays the French horn."

"Romeo Farina," we all moaned.

Looking over at the cardboard figure that still commanded a corner of our classroom, Miss Boland threw a rather daring wink. Some of the girls giggled, until a warning glance from Miss Kelly reminded us that we were still in school and still supposed to be on our best behavior.

"It's true that we're all excited," said Miss Kelly, "now that school's almost over, and so much is scheduled for the Fourth of July . . . yet we shall *all* remain in control of our manners."

"Oh," said Miss Boland, "I can't wait."

Miss Kelly, in her dry voice that she usually used only once a day, said, "Neither can I."

"I hope," said Miss Boland, "that Romeo . . . I mean Mr. Farina . . . will be able to spot me in the crowd."

Soup whispered, "Spot her? She *is* the crowd."

"Now don't forget, children. Band practice at three today, like always," said our nurse. "And also tomorrow."

"And Wednesday too?"

"*No!* Wednesday is train day."

Wednesday arrived.

So did the Green Mountain Limited. At least a half hour prior to its being due, much of the town had already gathered at the railroad station. We stood in the boiling sun, squinted southward, seeing only an empty track. Then our cocked ears were rewarded by a distant whistle. Puffs of black smoke billowed closer and closer. Giant wheels screamed to a stop. A conductor in a blue uniform with a hundred gold buttons got off the daycoach first, planting a footstool for the one passenger to dismount.

Miss Boland waved her hanky.

And then the one passenger appeared, tipping his white Panama hat to the adoring faces. Coming down the steps, he grew shorter and shorter until neither Soup nor

I could spot him anymore. We had to shinny up the posts of the railroad station even to see his face.

It looked to Soup and me that the man who had come to town was about *half* of Mr. Romeo Farina.

nine

"Rob!"

I heard somebody calling my name, but I didn't want to hear it. That was because I was dreaming my favorite dream, the one where I ride up on a white horse and rescue Norma Jean Bissell from a dangerous band of train robbers.

The leader of the criminals, in my dream, was usually Janice Riker.

"Wake up, Rob."

I wouldn't wake up. Because now I was boarding the

runaway train, and the engineer was Mr. Romeo Farina. The train didn't have a whistle. Only a French horn. And fireworks were shooting red, white, and blue stars out of the smokestack. All that plus Norma Jean wearing a dress like Miss Boland's. For some reason I was in a pink band uniform and the racing locomotive sounded like Big Boy, my gigantic new drum.

"Rob!"

My eyes opened.

Stumbling over to my bedroom window, I looked out into the moonlight. Down on the ground, Soup was standing, fully clothed.

"Come on," he was saying.

"Are you crazy?" I asked Soup. "It's the middle of the night. The parade's not until tomorrow."

"I got a nifty idea," whispered Soup, moving a step closer to being beneath my upstairs window.

As he said "idea," a shudder rattled along my spine, like a warning. "Don't go" ordered my backbone, as well as my brain. Soup's ideas, especially when they come to him at midnight, spell nothing but trouble.

"We'll try it out tomorrow," I said. Miss Boland had marched us around and around the Grange Hall all day, so I felt rather sleepy.

"Quiet," warned Soup, "or you'll wake your Aunt Carrie."

Soup was right. In the middle of the night, if somebody sneezed in Phoenix, Arizona, my aunt would wake up, trot up and down the upstairs hall in her nightie, and yell, "What was that?" Nighttime, to her, was sentry duty.

"Get dressed," said Soup.

"Where are we going? No, I don't mean that. What I mean is . . . where are *you* off to?"

Soup whispered, "The baseball park."

"At *this* hour?"

"I gotta," Soup insisted. "It's the only solution."

"To what?"

"So," said Soup, "I can get even with Janice."

Janice Riker, I was thinking . . . that bullyish train robber who had made much of my schoolyard life a variety show of bumps and bruises. Not to mention red, black, and blue. With old Janice around, by the end of the summer every kid in town would look more colorful than the American flag.

"What's your plan, Soup?"

"I'll explain on the way. You coming?"

Taking a deep breath, and hoping Aunt Carrie would wake up and order me to remain in the comfort of my bed, I nodded.

"Don't bother to put your clothes on," said Soup, who was fully dressed. "It's hot out."

Wearing only the bottoms of my pajamas, the lavender ones with the long rip up the knee, I eased myself out the window and across the roof. Down the drainpipe, grabbing a tree, I joined Soup on the ground below. My bare feet bit the dust. "Are you sure we won't get in trouble?"

"Impossible," said Soup.

"How come? We always do."

"Because," said Soup.

I was too tired to dispute his logic. Soup was right. It was one hot night, yet, for some strange cause, we ran most of the way to the ballpark. Soup wore his sneakers. I was barefoot.

"What's your big idea, Soup?"

"Fireworks."

It had better be nothing less, I was thinking as I stopped to pull a burdock pricker out of my toe, than blowing up Janice.

"Here we are," said Soup.

I yawned.

Soup said, "And now the rest'll be easy."

"How easy?"

"A leadpipe cinch."

"Well, whatever it is, let's do it and get done. Tomorrow's the Fourth of July and my mother told me I'd best get a good night's sleep."

Soup nodded. "Yeah, my mom said the same thing. Did yours say . . . you've got a big day tomorrow?"

"Yes," I said. "Exactly."

"Mothers are all alike," said Soup. "It's like they all sort of studied motherhood out of the same manual."

"We're wasting time, Soup. Whatever it is you want to do, let's have at it."

"Patience," answered Soup. Pulling a folded piece of

yellow paper from his pants pocket, he carefully unfolded it, holding it under the moonlight.

"What's that?" I asked.

"Nothing."

"Looks like a homework paper."

Soup shot me a grin. "Well, it sort of is. Even though school's over, we can teach old Janice a lesson."

"Okay," I said. "Spill it."

"Rob, do you recall that photograph the Super-Sweet Fireworks guy was showing us?"

"Sort of."

"My idea," said Soup, "is to create a new arrangement out in center field."

"Huh?"

"Come on."

Center field was a crowded place. Big letters, held up by wires, one of which I tripped over, stretched out in the darkness. My bare foot fell on the rim of a belly-up bottle cap.

"Ouch!"

"Quiet," whispered Soup.

"I just stepped on a bottle cap."

"We don't have time for that now," said Soup. "Not if we're going to get even with Janice."

"Are you sure that's what we're doing?"

"Yup," said Soup. "I'm certain sure."

"Okay," I said, limping among the giant letters that had been carefully planted to spell out:

I LOVE A SUPER-SWEET FOURTH OF JULY.

"Now what?" I asked Soup.

Luther Wesley Vinson squinted at his crumpled paper. "First," he said, "we borrow this big S."

Pulling up the stakes that had the wires anchored to the ground, we moved the S over toward left field. It was a bit heftier, Soup admitted, than he had counted on. Moving letters this size was one heck of a grunt.

"Okay," I panted at Soup. "What's next?"

We lugged another letter that Soup had selected. My foot was hurting, and more, a mosquito was really chawing away on my bare back. The moon was behind a cloud, and the night darkened to an inky and eerie blackness.

"Golly," I said, "this is a heavy load. Which letter is it?"

"A love letter," Soup giggled.

People who smash pop bottles in ballparks, I was thinking as my foot found some glass, ought to really get theirs. My hand slapped at another bug which was making a meal out of my chest. I thought I also heard a slight rip.

"And now," Soup happily announced, "for a V."

Secretly, I hoped the V wouldn't be as heavy as the O we'd just moved. But it was.

Soup was whistling.

I didn't much like the sound of his music. If there's one thing I can't stand in the middle of the night, with a cut foot and bug bites, it's *happiness*. Especially as it was all Soup's.

We moved more letters, including a big *J*.

"Soup . . ."

"Yeah?"

"Are we spelling Janice?"

"Uh, sort of . . . but not exactly, if you know what I mean. Trust me."

"I want to know *now* what we're doing. If you're spelling out dirty words, I don't want to be a part of it."

"Hey," said Soup, "don't worry so much."

"Then why don't I ever get to look at what's written down on your paper?"

"Well," said Soup, "it's sort of a surprise."

"You mean like the drum."

Soup nodded. "Sort of like that, only bigger. Rob, nudge the bottom over more. It looks a mite crooked."

I nudged it.

"No," said Soup, "that's too much. Best you haul it back a couple of inches."

It sure was hot! Sweat was streaming down my brow, and the salt was smarting my eyes. More mosquitoes stung my body. Dark as it was, I couldn't see what I was doing, and I was starting to care less and less about how I was getting even with Janice Riker. Letter after letter was tugged.

The big *E* we lugged weighed near a ton. In school, I really had never warmed up to spelling a whole lot. But this job had to be about the warmest I'd ever been. Soup held the paper while I moved the letters, swatted, sweated, and swore.

"Are you sure," I asked Soup, "that Janice isn't home in bed getting even with *us*?"

"Just you wait," chuckled Soup.

"To me, all the big letters didn't seem to be in any order at all. My foot was hurting, my body itching, my arms aching, and I wanted to go home.

"Are we done yet?"

"Almost," said Soup. "One more letter."

"Which one?"

"This one," said Soup. "All we need now is to untangle the *T* out of this bunch and tote it over to ours."

"Okay, but there isn't any *T* in Janice." I was enough of a speller to figure that out, but seeing as we'd come this far, it would be a crime to quit now. Maybe, I thought, it was already a crime to do what we were doing. Would we both get caught and end up in jail?

"There," said Soup with a final sigh.

"Don't tell me we're finished."

Soup nodded. "We're all done."

"Thank the good gosh," I said, sinking to the soft grass of center field. My pajamas must have been rotten because I heard one powerful rip. A real zipper.

"Now," said Soup, "all we have to do is hide the letters we haven't used."

"*Hide?*"

"Yep," said Soup. "All part of my plan."

Somehow, through bugs and sweat and more upturned bottle caps, we lugged away the extra letters. Thirteen in all. I had no idea which ones they were and cared even less. My pajamas were now so badly torn that they fell down with almost every step. I was swatting bugs with one hand and trying to cover up my bare bottom with the other.

"One more task," said Soup, "and we can call it quits for tonight."

"No. I can't do any more."

"Sure you can, Rob."

"Darn it," I told Soup, "it's easy for *you* to talk. You got sneakers on your feet. All I got to wear is what my mother always says, 'We'll make a dustrag out of it.' But there's not enough left of my pajama pants to dust off a jelly bean."

"Don't complain," said Soup. "If there's anything I can't abide, it's a fusser."

"Let's go home, Soup."

"Okay, as soon as we hook up the fuse cables, sort of like they were before."

"How?"

"Each letter ought to be attached to the next. Nothing to it. I figure we just twist the cables around in a knot. Bare end to bare end."

I looked for the cable's bare end just as the hungriest mosquito in Vermont found mine.

ten

"Form up," ordered Miss Boland.

Nineteen pink uniforms stumbled and fumbled in milling confusion outside the Grange Hall, as we all tried to remember our proper positions for marching.

It was almost seven o'clock in the evening, and I could hardly wait for the parade to start so that Norma Jean Bissell could see me and my drum. Big Boy was harnessed to my back, and behind the big bass drum, Soup was holding it up from the rear. We had rigged up a second harness for him. Soup held a drumbeater in each hand. We had decided it would be easier for him to beat the drum. Earlier I had tried marching backwards with the drum held at my front, in order to beat Big Boy, but I tripped too often.

"Perhaps," said Miss Boland, "the autoharp ought to march between the glockenspiel and the triangle."

From where I stood, my giant bass drum was between me and Soup. I had my back to him and the drum, but I felt the drum swing a bit to the left every time he turned to smile at Juliet Rapture. Her pink band uniform, I decided, hadn't improved her redheaded looks any. It sure was hard for me to understand Soup's idea of beauty.

"Well," growled Mr. Jubert, "where is he?"

Miss Webster, our town librarian, who was warming up on her harmonica, stopped playing to look at Mr. Jubert. "Where's who?"

"That there Farina feller, that Frenchman who's suppose to play the Italian horn."

I looked around for Mr. Romeo Farina, who, according to Miss Boland, had agreed to march as a band member in our Fourth of July parade. He sure was a good sport.

"Well, I don't see him," said Miss Webster. "By the way, we never did decide on what piece we'd play first."

Mr Jubert smiled over his fiddle. "Yep, we decided. And I'm happy to say, despite the protests of that dangfool trombone player, that the first number we play is 'Honolulu Baby'."

With his trombone, Mr. Petty made a disgusting noise, as though his instrument suffered from some kind of gastric distress.

Miss Boland, who was wearing her new dress, dashed inside the Grange Hall. I wondered why. Moments later, she reappeared, but not in her flowery dress. She now wore an outfit that made her dress seem drab by

94

comparison. Miss Boland had put on a drum-majorette's uniform that was redder than fire, and trimmed with silver and gold spangles, topped off by a white bearskin hat that added an extra twenty inches to her height. On top of the hat was a pink plume. Instead of her clarinet, she now waved a silver baton that was longer than a pitchfork, one end of which sported a sparkling gold ball that was near the size of a melon.

"That woman," I overheard Mr. Jubert mutter, "must think she's our new fire truck."

Then I spotted an even more sorrowful sight. Trotting toward the Grange Hall, I saw the twentieth pink uniform, inside which was probably a human being. Hard to tell for sure, as the uniform was several sizes too large for its occupant.

"Who's that?" asked Miss Webster. "And what's that contraption he's carrying?"

Miss Boland smiled broadly from beneath her enormous headgear. "That," she announced, "is a French horn."

Somewhere inside the oversized pink uniform was Mr. Romeo Farina. Yet all I could see of him was the hook of his nose and a tiny black mustache. Beneath the mustache, a mouth suddenly smiled.

"Miss Boland," he said. "Farina is ready."

None of us fitted our uniforms too well. In fact, Mr. Horrace Jubert's pink trousers covered only the upper three quarters of his long legs. He was also wearing one blue sock and one of pale green.

Everyone wanted to march next to Mr. Farina, which turned out to be impossible, as Miss Boland quickly pointed out. Finally, it was agreed that Mr. Farina would march in the front row, between Mr. Petty's trombone and Mr. Bissell's saxophone.

Soup and I, hitched forward and aft to Big Boy, were once again ordered to the rear, as Miss Boland explained, for the tenth time, that all twenty of us couldn't very well march in the front row. There would, Miss Boland computed, be five rows of marchers, four abreast.

"Can't we get started with the parade?" I asked. "This drum weighs a ton."

I kept wondering how much of Big Boy old Soup was holding up. Half? Soup had told me that the front half was lighter, especially going uphill. Well, I thought, at least I'm the leader, up in front of the drum where Norma Jean Bissell would see me as we proudly paraded down Main Street. Right now, however, we were still not lined up properly enough.

"Now then," said Miss Boland, "the autoharp ought to be repositioned in the third row, between the cymbals and the ukulele."

"Over here?" asked Aunt Carol.

"No," shouted Miss Boland, *"over there!"*

It was then that Mr. Dumas Mack, our oldest member, lifted his Spanish-American War bugle to his talented lips and started to blow "Over There."

"You folks ready?"

Looking up, I saw another uniform. Not pink, but

96

olive drab, the color worn by our Home Guard. The man who wore it also had wraparound leggings, orange boots, and a steel half-helmet. I recognized him. It was Mr. Rank Delaney. On his olive-drab chest was pinned some sort of a medal, which strangely resembled my Orphan Annie Club ribbon.

"We're ready," said Miss Boland.

"Good," said Mr. Delaney. "Now, if you don't mind, the Home Guard will *lead* the parade, and next . . ."

"I mind," said Miss Boland.

"Why?"

"Because the Home Guard has led the parade every year. Now we've got a band, let's lead off with one of our rousing marches."

"Now look here," said Mr. Delaney, "we fellows practice marching darn near every Tuesday night, at the Armory. So when it comes to parading, we're professionals."

"Maybe," said Miss Boland. "But you fellows in the Home Guard still have Wheeler."

"You mean Wheeler Powell?"

"I don't mean Wheeler Dealer. That gink's *never* been able to march as far as the outhouse without falling down, and you know it, Rank."

Mr. Delaney snorted. Eyeing the members of our band, he abruptly pointed at one of our pink uniforms. "Who's that?"

It was Miss Boland's turn to snort. "He happens to be one of our *star* performers, Mr. Romeo Farina.

"And who's *that* over there?"

"Where?"

"In the second row. That person's not even carrying an instrument."

"Oh," said Miss Boland, "she's our vocalist, Mrs. Stetson."

"Never heard of a singer in a band."

"We were missing a piccolo," explained Miss Boland with a shrug of her gold-braided shoulders, "so Mrs. Stetson sort of fills in the trills."

"Oh yeah? What piece are you playing first?"

" 'Honolulu Baby.' "

"That's hillbilly music."

"Told ya so," said Mr. Petty.

"Look," said Mr. Delaney, "it really doesn't matter what *order* we're in, long as we all get to march."

"You're right, Rank."

"Good, then . . ."

"We'll go first," said Miss Boland.

"Ladies first," said Miss Webster.

"Okay," said Mr. Delaney, "but don't forget the route."

"We won't."

"First we leave the Grange Hall and turn the corner at the red light, then up Main Street, past the schoolhouse, and finish up at the ballpark."

"That's quite a ways," said Miss Boland.

Mr. Petty agreed. "Sure is, in this heat. I don't guess I ever recall a Fourth of July any hotter than the one we got this evening."

Just then, Gale Pinder, our local fire chief, trotted our way, dressed in his blue marching trousers, a white undershirt, and his red fire helmet.

"We got trouble."

"What's the problem, Gale?"

"Seems like we pulled the hose out of the new fire truck, just to see how long she measured, and we can't seem to fold her up the way she came."

Mr. Rank Delaney scowled at Chief Pinder. "That's the trouble with you volunteer firemen. No discipline."

"Yeah? Well, I could say the same about what you soldier boys call a Home Guard."

"Sez you."

"I wouldn't trust a one of ya to guard a radish."

"Boys," said Miss Boland, "we'd best get started, else it'll be dark, and we won't get to the ballpark in time to view the fireworks show."

"Ah," said Chief Pinder, "that reminds me. There's a local statute that says no fireworks will be exploded inside the incorporation without a *trained fire expert* on hand. Unless there is, they can't shoot off a thing."

"If you ask me," said Mr. Petty, "the only thing you ever shoot off is your big mouth."

"I'll ignore that," said Chief Pinder, "on account of we're running late. Say, I got an idea! In the parade, the fire truck ought to go first."

As he said it, our fire chief smiled at Miss Boland and Mr. Delaney of the Home Guard. And then everybody was smiling.

"Done," said Miss Boland.

"Yup," said Rank, "the fire truck will lead off."

"And then the band," suggested our big and bright-red majorette.

Right then, we all took our positions behind the new fire truck that was still trailing its extra thirty feet of hose. But nobody seemed to give a hoot, as even the faces of most of our volunteer firefighters wore smiles—and red noses. Several members, it appeared, had been celebrating the Fourth of July with liquid refreshment.

Our parade inched forward, fire truck foremost.

"Be careful," hollered Miss Boland, "and don't anybody step on the hose."

Three sharp blasts on Miss Boland's whistle gave the signal. Our snare drum, beneath the able sticks of Mr. Diskin, rolled out a rousing rhythm which Soup, from behind my drum, followed by booming Big Boy. My drum felt heavier with each step, but I wasn't going to quit . . . not until we reached the ballpark.

Rounding the corner by the traffic light, the new fire engine wheeled up Main Street. People lined the sidewalk, cheering, waving to their marching friends and neighbors. Furtively I looked for Norma Jean Bissell.

All I saw was Janice Riker, throwing a rotten egg at the fire truck and sticking out her tongue. There was a kid who really knew how to make herself popular. But when she spotted Soup, her scowl brightened into a grin, and she blew him a kiss.

She yelled, "Look at Soup's drum!"

Soup's drum? Something was going wrong. Big Boy

was *my* drum. After all, wasn't I the guy marching in front of it, carrying it on my back? Oh well, I then remembered, Janice didn't always get everything right.

Miss Boland blew her whistle again.

Mr. Diskin changed his snare beat, which prompted about half of our band to wade into "Honolulu Baby." The rest of them seemed undecided, as if trying to choose between "It's a Grand Old Flag" and "Juanita." But I'll say this for Mr. Dumas Mack; he wasn't at all at a loss as to *his* selection. Bugle up, he blasted out his loudest rendition of "Over There."

We really didn't sound like a band. It was more like a factory.

Mr. Romeo Farina turned and yelled out something to our bugler, in Italian, making a gesture with his hands that didn't appear too appreciative. It was then that Miss Boland dropped her baton, and Mr. Farina, swearing over his shoulder at our bugler, crashed into Miss Boland just as she bent over to recapture it.

Several other events rapidly followed: Mr. Petty dropped his music book. Miss Webster, our librarian, fell over Mr. Petty. Half the band broke ranks to avoid further disaster, but then tripped on the hose, which somehow entwined its nozzle around Mr. Farina's ankle. A string snapped on Mr. Jubert's fiddle. The hose yanked Mr. Farina, French horn and all, into Mrs. Stetson, who swore . . . and it sure wasn't in Italian.

One by one, and in our own casual way, we stopped playing "Honolulu Baby."

eleven

I grunted.

Had I not known that I was carrying my big drum up Main Street, I could have sworn that I was toting Miss Boland . . . across Egypt. Why, I asked myself, are parades always uphill?

Soup and I marched slower and slower. We were about halfway through town when I realized that the rest of the band had left us behind. We were now marching with a group of women in orange and white uniforms, the Methodist Daughters. I only discovered this because, with a superhuman effort, I lifted my head. Big Boy was so heavy I'd been looking down at the road.

"Where's our band?" Soup hollered to me from behind our big drum. Funny, he didn't sound nearly as tired as I felt.

"Up ahead," I answered. "In front of Mr. Delaney and the rest of the Home Guard."

Soup said, "Best we run and catch up."

"*Run?* I can hardly walk. This doggone tom-tom weighs a ton, and we still haven't seen Norma Jean Bissell."

We ran. Not because I wanted to, but because Soup began pushing from the rear. We jogged our way through the Home Guard and were once again part of the band, back in formation. We were just in time to hear an argument.

During our absence, a new member had joined.

Wheeler Powell, holding his flag on high, now marched between Miss Webster and Mrs. Stetson. The band had changed its order. Our front row was now comprised of only Miss Boland and Mr. Romeo Farina. Oddly enough, seven bandsmen marched in the fourth row; Soup and I rejoined the last-row stragglers.

"Let's play," suggested Mr. Jubert.

Mrs. Stetson said, "Whispering Hope." She began to sing it in her wavering soprano. Her voice fluttered like Wheeler Powell's flag.

Unfortunately, we had failed to discuss the second number of our presentation, so the upshot of the matter was we again played "Honolulu Baby." Except for Mrs. Stetson . . . and for Mr. Dumas Mack, who was bugling (and bungling) "Retreat." It sounded like he was blowing with only one lip.

I saw Norma Jean Bissell.

She didn't seem to notice me. Her eyes seemed to be watching Soup, even though Big Boy was *mine*. As we passed by, I heard her remark, "Look at Soup's drum."

Suddenly I didn't want to get even with Janice Riker. All I ached to do was settle a score with Luther Wesley Vinson. Had I not been helplessly buckled inside that harness, I would have turned around and laced him proper. The very thought of that term . . . *Soup's drum* . . . made me boil up pinker than my uniform.

"Halt," hollered Miss Boland, along with a sharp blast of her whistle.

Whew! We'd made it to the ballpark. Kneeling, I rested the drum on the ground. It was a good thing that the proposed route of our Fourth of July parade had not been one inch longer, or I never would have lasted. I was wet with sweat.

"We made it," said Soup.

Struggling free of my drum harness, I looked around at Soup, who appeared fresher than paint. He wasn't even pink in the cheeks, or winded.

Several girls ran up to us, telling Soup how *wonderful* he was in the parade, and that they never *knew* he was such an accomplished drummer. They even had the nerve to use the term *Soup's drum* about a hundred times.

"It's *my* drum," I said.

But nobody heard.

"Keep back, folks."

Turning, I saw Mr. Rank Delaney holding a long unlit

torch plus a box of safety matches. It was just getting dark.

Bombs exploded.

We all covered our ears. All of us, that is, with the one exception of Wheeler Powell, who continued to march around the ballpark, eyes upward, revering his flag. Soup was busy hiding from Janice Riker, who had spotted him and was blowing kisses.

"Somehow," said Soup, "I liked her a whole lot better when she *hated* me."

I looked around for Norma Jean Bissell, but she was nowhere to be found. Besides, I was really too tuckered out to care. How we'd ever get Big Boy back to the Grange was a rather discomforting thought. Darn it! I sure wasn't intending to tote *Soup's drum* one more step.

Miss Boland blew her whistle. "And now," she announced when almost everyone was attentive, "Mr. Romeo Farina has consented to do us the honor of rendering a solo. On the French horn."

There was scattered applause.

Smiling at the crowd, Mr. Farina silently fingered his horn, in preparation. But then he scowled as old Mr. Dumas Mack had already begun to bugle "First Call," along with one or two borrowed passages from "Mexicali Rose."

Mr. Farina finally played, a brilliant performance of "Lady of Spain I Adore You," followed by something that had to do with a sweet nutcracker. I didn't quite catch the name. During his last and final note on the French horn, one more Super-Sweet bomb exploded, making everyone jump and Mr. Farina furious. He said some irate words, in Italian, to Mr. Rank Delaney.

I spotted Miss Kelly and waved to her. She walked over to where I sat, still puffing, on the edge of Big Boy. As she approached, I stood up, the way Mama and Aunt Carrie always told me to do.

"Robert," said Miss Kelly, "you must be exhausted."

"Yes'm," I admitted, "I sure am."

"How you carried Soup's drum I'll never know."

That, I decided, was the lethal blow. I was going to get even with Soup if it took the rest of the summer. But how? Just as I was giving this noble project full thought, I saw Janice Riker. She was handily beating up Eddy Tacker, the second-toughest kid at school. Eddy finally got loose and ran off.

"Janice," I yelled.

"Yeah?" Her fists were still doubled.

"Watch out for Soup."

"How come?"

"He's going to kiss you, Janice."

"No, he ain't. I'm going to kiss *him* first."

Skyrockets were fired off.

Wheeler Powell was still marching, knees high, around and around the ballpark, waving the American flag. Somewhere, from the midst of the crowd, I thought I heard Mrs. Stetson singing "The Star Spangled Banner." Several men removed their hats.

I saw Janice. Looking, no doubt, for Soup.

Mama, Papa, and Aunt Carrie were there at the ballpark and bought me a cold root beer. It sure was gassy, and the bubbles stung my nose.

Half the band, mostly the grown-ups, had enjoyed more than root beer and were now attempting one last rendition of "Honolulu Baby." Earlier hostilities seemed to have healed, as Mr. Jubert and Mr. Petty draped their arms about each other's shoulders and were singing a duet . . . "Home on the Range."

"We can't do the grand finale," complained Rank Delaney, "unless they move the fire truck."

Several events unfolded:

Chief Pinder, who was now wearing his fire helmet backward, started the new red fire truck. But instead of pulling forward, he threw the gears into reverse. The big engine backed into Mr. Rank Delaney, who was holding his burning torch. Rank stumbled into the letters Soup and I had rearranged.

The torch touched a fuse, and *poof!* A large S ignited, spraying sparks and stars and smoke . . . in red, white, blue, purple and gold.

Mrs. Stetson screamed.

The hose once again fell off the fire truck, along with Chief Pinder and several other celebrating volunteers. Soup, without my help, began to pound Big Boy, as though trying to get everyone's attention, especially Juliet's.

Dumas Mack bugled "Mess Call." And it sure was a mess.

With its gears grinding, our new fire truck charged in a forward direction, bumping Mrs. Stetson and Miss Webster, who fell over on Big Boy. I heard a rip. The ancient drumhead gave way and was thoroughly destroyed. It looked like an empty can of cat food. Hollow and forlorn, it now could only be played on one side. I tipped it up on its edge, sort of in a rolling position, to look inside.

Mr. Jubert, for some reason, was tooting the slide trombone, while Mr. Petty had switched over to the fiddle. The spit valve on the trombone slide somehow got tangled up in the lanyard on the fire engine, and blew the siren.

More letters burst into flame.

"Hey!" yelled Rank Delaney. "Something's wrong."

Wheeler Powell became overly excited, running through the crowd, flag on high. Until he tripped on a wire. I saw the tip of his flagpole ram into Miss Boland's behind. Lurching forward, she crashed into Mr. Farina, who was playing "Chloe." His hand was jammed into the bell of his French horn and he hollered a few European phrases, more colorful than Wheeler's flag.

"Wow!" I pointed at the exploding letters. "I don't believe it. Look!"

SOUP LOVES JULIET burned in red, white, blue, purple and gold—emblazened into the night sky.

Even though it was dark out, every surprised face in town was lit up, as every pair of eyes read the letters that had originally been intended to form I LOVE A

SUPER-SWEET FOURTH OF JULY.

Janice, who could spell almost as cleverly as our cow, Daisy, was smiling. Apparently, old Janice couldn't read the difference between *her* name and Juliet's. I don't guess she saw much more of the burning name except the J.

"I love you too, Luther!" yelled Janice.

Soup never had a chance.

Before you could say "Soup loves Juliet," old Janice jumped all over Soup and began to smother him with a barrage of kisses. Her determined lips sounded like a sink plunger unplugging a clogged drain.

Soup was screaming bloody murder.

Yet he wasn't hollering even half as loud as Mr. Farina, because Miss Boland, Mrs. Stetson, and Miss Webster were trying, unsuccessfully, to yank his hand out of the bell of his French horn.

Soup was down . . . Janice on top of him. That was when I ran over to where they were kissing (mostly it was Janice kissing) and got the best idea in my whole life. There, beside them, stood Big Boy, missing one of its sides.

With a quick heave, I tipped over Soup's drum, so that now Janice and Soup were underneath, inside Big Boy. From where I was, up on top to weight it down, I could still hear Janice kissing and Soup yelling for help.

"Serves ya right," I said.

From the corner of my eyes, I spotted Juliet Rapture,

still in her pink band uniform, looking for Soup. She was calling, "Luther!"

She came close. "Rob, have you seen Soup?"

"I don't see him anywhere," I said.

Right then, in order to muffle the screams and kisses from inside the drum, I picked up the two potato-masher drumsticks Soup had used and began to beat Big Boy's good side (the side that was *up*) with all my might.

Juliet Rapture looked at me as though slightly confused. "How come you're playing Soup's drum?"

I laughed. "Juliet," I said, still pounding Big Boy with both sticks, "it's a long story."

She wandered off. SOUP LOVES JULIET was slowly burning out, but the crowd was clapping their hands in awe and appreciation of the grand finale.

Then the best part happened.

Norma Jean Bissell came over. Together we sat on the flat circular face of the big bass drum, while I continued to thump Big Boy with what little strength I still had.

Norma Jean said, "Rob, I think you're a better drummer than Soup."

"Thanks," I said.

SOUP LOVES JULIET, the romance that had set Vermont aflame, burned out.

As it was now dark once again, and no one was looking or caring, Norma Jean Bissell leaned over and kissed my cheek. And I kissed hers. Then, mustering up renewed courage, I kissed her softly on the lips. *Boom!* My heart pounded louder than Soup's drum, which I continued to beat.

It sure turned out to be a peachy Fourth of July, sitting on Big Boy with Norma Jean Bissell, and knowing Soup was down inside, helplessly in the headlock of Janice Riker.

Soup's drum, I thought, would certain be *one* drum he'd always remember.

"You're getting better," whispered Norma Jean.

"At kissing?" I asked her.

"No," she said. "At drumming."